Anonymous

Out of School at Eton

Being a Collection of Poetry and Prose Writings

Anonymous

Out of School at Eton
Being a Collection of Poetry and Prose Writings

ISBN/EAN: 9783337086398

Printed in Europe, USA, Canada, Australia, Japan

Cover: Foto ©Andreas Hilbeck / pixelio.de

More available books at **www.hansebooks.com**

OUT OF SCHOOL AT ETON.

LONDON :
GILBERT AND RIVINGTON, PRINTERS,
ST. JOHN'S SQUARE.

OUT OF SCHOOL AT ETON.

BEING

A COLLECTION OF POETRY AND PROSE WRITINGS

By SOME PRESENT ETONIANS.

" Liberius si
Dixero quid, si forte jocosius, hoc mihi juris
Cum venia dabis."

HORACF, Sat. I. 4.

London :

SAMPSON LOW, MARSTON, SEARLE, & RIVINGTON,

CROWN BUILDINGS, 188, FLEET STREET.

1877.

PREFACE.

THIS little book is what its title sets it forth to be, viz. a collection of miscellaneous writings with the composition of which we Eton boys have from time to time occupied our leisure hours. Several of them were printed in *The Etonian*, a literary paper which flourished here about a year ago ; but a number have not yet appeared in print, and are now indeed for the first time brought together. The numerous requests made to us to republish some of the former in the more connected shape of a book, first induced us to think of venturing on the step which we have now taken; and the support which has been promised us in the case of our doing so, will we hope justify the somewhat ambitious attempt. At the same time we trust that the idea of our work will commend itself to our readers, inasmuch as it is from a desire to prove that literary talent, or at any rate literary spirit, is not extinct at Eton, and that Eton boys can find interest in other occupations than the mere ordinary routine of work and play, that we have overcome the diffidence which we naturally feel at submitting our endeavour to the eyes of the public.

Our readers will we hope excuse the miscellaneous character of our writings, and the promiscuous manner in which they have been brought together, but the task of arranging them in a more careful manner is one which from our inexperience we have shrunk from undertaking. It seemed better to us, on the whole, to present them just as we wrote them, with here and there an explanatory note, and to trust to the good nature of those under whose notice they may come, to excuse all minor faults and deficiencies, and to take our book for what it is worth as an attempt, the first which has been made for many years, to vindicate the literary prestige of Eton.

THE WRITERS.

Eton, *May*, 1877.

CONTENTS.

OUT OF SCHOOL AT ETON.

AN HOUR OF MY LIFE AT ETON.

I SAID before I went to bed
    At half-past six I'd rise,
But, as in some strange book I've read,
Things can't be done by being said,
    And there the moral lies.

For all the things that overnight
    Did most important seem,
Are trifles view'd by morning's light,
And early school is alter'd quite
    Into a hideous dream.

For what on earth's the use "to post
    With such dexterity "
(You see I'm quoting from the Ghost
In Hamlet) where no butter'd toast,
    No coffee waits for me?

B

Such thoughts as these went through my brain
   When half-past six did strike;
I felt that it would give me pain
In bed no longer to remain,
   For rest I greatly like.

In short then, when at last I rose,
   I felt I'd play'd the fool,
That I'd enjoy'd too long a doze,
In fine that (as the saying goes)
   I should be late for school.

I might have been in time, but that
   (I am not telling lies)
I dropp'd my shirt and boots and hat
Into my bath; and then a rat
   Had eaten all my ties.

     *   *   *   *   *

"Good! dress'd at last!" I madly cried,
   And rush'd from out my room;
But Fate was present at my side,
And down the stairs with headlong slide
   To tumble was my doom.

My hands and knees were badly cut,
   My trousers torn to rags,   ·
I hardly felt in spirits, but
I rose, and with a hasty " Tut!
   Why should I mind my *bags ?*"

I made for school ; without a tie,
   Without a hat, in vain
With utmost wariness I try
To 'scape the master's eagle eye,
   And spare him useless pain.

I'd all but reach'd the long'd-for place,
   When lo ! a luckless sneeze
Betray'd me ; o'er my teacher's face
There pass'd a horrible grimace,
   Then came such words as these :—

" For daring to come in without
   First putting on a tie,
You'll have the goodness to appear
At one and five throughout the year ;
   Who's master, you or I ?
And "—he pursued, with brutal shout—
" For being late you'll write me out
   ' Poetæ Scenici.' "

THE HORSE.

Vide " The Brook," by Tennyson.

WITH many a curve my legs I set
  In many a field and fallow,
In many a miry meadow wet
  With willow-weed and mallow,

I slip, I slide, I scrape, I glance,
  As on the road I straddle,
I make my worthy master dance
  Upon his well-worn saddle.

And on again in gallant show
  Along the road I quiver,
For men ride fast, and men ride slow,
  But I jog on for ever.

Without a doubt I scramble out
  Through many a ditch and railing,
With here and there an " in and out,"
  And here and there a paling ;

And here and there a foamy flake
  Upon me as I travel,
And here and there a heavy shake
  From tumbling on the gravel ;

But up again without a blow,
  I dash across the river,
For men ride fast, and men ride slow,
  But I jog on for ever.

I steal by lawns and grassy plots,
  I slide by foxes' covers,
I crush the sweet forget-me-nots
  That grow for happy lovers.

I murmur under moon and stars
  In brambly wildernesses,
Which tear the skin from off my tail,
  And add to my distresses.

I clatter, clatter, as I go
  Beside the brimming river,
For men ride fast, and men ride slow,
  But I jog on for ever.

———

THE CRITIC'S SPEECH.

" JUST the book to review !" the critic cried
(The Chase of the Snark, to wit),

While his audience press'd round him on every
    side,
  To hear his opinion of it.

" They read it with glasses, they read it with
    care,
  They peruse it again and again,
They ruin their health beyond repair,
  And they give themselves Snark on the brain.

" But what are the charms of this curious tale,
  Which attract such a numerous band,
Or why it obtains so extensive a sale,
  I could never at all understand.

" The reader who looks through his various
    books,
  Five characteristics will mark,
Which always belong, both in prose and in song,
  To the author of ' Hunting the Snark.'

  " The first is the binding : especially that
    Of the book we presume to review,
  On which is depicted a watery flat
    Of a sickly cadaverous hue.

" That he's most inconsistent, I think you'll agree,
  When he dares to assert it as true,
That the rudder gets mix'd with the bowsprit at
    sea,
  Or that birds can be salted in glue.

" The third is his manner of making a jest,
  Which is quite and entirely his own,
And he seeks after witty remarks with a zest
  That might find the philosopher's stone.

" The fourth is the way that he sticks to a word
  (Such as beamish, galumph, and the rest),
Which he thinks is amusing as well as absurd,
  An opinion I beg to contest.

" The fifth is pure folly.   It now will be just
  To describe each particular vein,
Distinguishing 'fits' which appal and disgust,
  From 'fits' which are simply inane.

" For though much is as pointless as can be
    desired,
  I'm exceedingly sorry to say
That Kenealy—" the critic abruptly retired,
  For his audience had melted away

OUR HOUSE DEBATING SOCIETY.

LEND me thy aid, thou goddess of wisdom, owl-
eyed Athena,
(Owl-eyed, or grey-eyed, or blue-eyed, what is
it to me or my printer?
All of them scan very well, and are back'd by
profoundest of scholars)
Aid thou my song, for I sing of the innermost
temple of wisdom,
Which as I take it is seen in my tutor's debating
society;
Hear (and digest if thou canst) how we had an
inaugural meeting,
How we discuss'd whether Mary of Scotland
was justly beheaded.
Rose to his feet, sonorous with far-flashing
eloquence; stop, though—
Shall I disclose? I will not; let our names be
buried for ever;
Let us go forth to the world without our distinguishing labels,—
Rose to his feet, and address'd us the opener,
prince of debaters,

Wit to amuse, and satire to crush, and facts to
confound us,

All the aids that an orator needs were his in
abundance :

" Mr. President " (humbly) " and gentlemen "
(soothingly), " hear me,"

(Voice upgathering strength as he speaks, like the
bellying canvas

Swell'd by the freshening breeze upon Thames,
the fairest of rivers)

" Hear me, I pray, and excuse, if the matter or
which I address you

Is not as fresh as it might be, yea, savoureth
somewhat of staleness.

Have I not deeply studied the works of the
peerless Sir Walter ?

Have I not read my Froude? look'd out the
unfortunate Mary

In Biographical Encyclopædias ? what could I
do more ?

Hear, then, the gleanings I bring you, and how I
support my opinion."

Not unambitious, you say, and yet not a whit
too ambitious ;

Would I could follow the rest of his well-deliver'd
oration ;

How he described the state of affairs, and the
　　chief of the statesmen ;
Gave us an eloquent list of the vices and eke of
　　the failings
Which he observed in Walsingham, Burleigh,
　　Elizabeth, Mary,　　.
Any one else of the era which he was engaged in
　　discussing ;
Ending an eloquent speech with an almost
　　inspired peroration,
Praising Elizabeth up to the skies, and excusing
　　her failings,
Knocking off Mary as murderess, traitress, and
　　justly beheaded.
Then he resumed his seat, while plaudits thun-
　　der'd around him,
Wiped his face with a sigh of relief, and eyed the
　　opposer
Just with a tinge of contempt and with infinite
　　self-approbation.
Painfully rose the opposer, with countenance
　　anxious and harass'd,
Stood undecided a moment, then plunged his
　　hands in his pockets,
Having decided the point, and discarded the only
　　positions

Other than this that he knew of ; he might have
  put them behind him,
Or have grasp'd the back of his chair, a most
  elegant posture,
But which involved a circuitous route for his
  chair or his person ;
So he discarded them both, and stood with his
  hands in his pockets.
His was a stammering speech—a speech full of
  amplest regrettings,
That so important a task had fallen to one so
  unworthy.
All of us shared his regret, as we did his relief
  when he ended,
Blurted out his opinion that Mary was strictly
  religious,
Beautiful, moral, and learned, and most unjustly
  beheaded.
He that spoke next was a member who thought
  he was made for the purpose
Of being placed in the chair of his tutor's debating society ;
He would have been such a president ; he was
  so eloquent, well-read ;
All his views so extended, his manner so truly
  majestic.

Somehow, however, the house had not made the
    most of its chances ;
Somebody else they delighted to honour, and he
    that I speak of
Found but a single vote in favour of his taking
    office
(Some people said that the candidate knew very
    well where it came from),
So he effected the god unmoved by the squabbles
    beneath him,
Dropp'd just a fragment or two of his inex-
    haustible wisdom,
Treated us calmly and patiently always to some-
    thing of this kind :—
" Nobody sees the point of this really impossible
    problem ;
None of you seem to observe the truly insoluble
    question
Lying beneath this apparently trumpery matter
    of Mary.
All of us know very well what these gentlemen
    tell us so fully ;
All of us know the date, and we know that it's
    very unpleasant
Having one's head cut off, and most injudicious
    of women

When they are tired of their husbands to blow
    them up in their castles.
But for the mighty question of which this
    manifestation
Is but the merest hint and offscouring—you all
    disregard it.
I, who regard it, am wholly unable to form an
    opinion ;
So with your leave I'll abstain from voting at
    all on the question."
Somehow the speech was a failure, and wasn't
    applauded as loudly
As might have been the case with a more com-
    plimentary speaker,
More so I mean to his hearers, and less to his
    own understanding.
If you should wonder at my reporting the follow-
    ing speeches,
You must remember that I am a lover of human
    nature,
And I would fain reproduce such perfectly typical
    efforts.
Here is one who rises and says in a tremulous
    manner,
" I must fully agree with the opener's able
    oration,

And I have nothing to add to his arguments ;"
here is another

Who must fully accord with his friend the enlighten'd opposer,

And who cannot improve on his manner of
treating the question.

Mark you the next that rises, a leader of taste
and refinement,

Intellectual he and æsthetic; scorner of clas-
sics

Studied with care or with notes; detester of
mathematics ;

Stern abjurer of rowing, of football, fives and
cricket ;

Faithful to Tennyson, Gladstone, Carlyle, and
Matthew Arnold ;

Great admirer of Ruskin ; peruser of pamphlets
and weeklies ;

Takes in the *Daily News* and Nineteenth Century; studies

Every taste in fact except those of playing and
working,

Which the authorities chiefly prefer in this centre
of darkness.

As for reporting his speech, I own that I couldn't
attempt it.

His is a jumble of all the styles of his favourite
    authors :
Lines out of Harold are side by side with pieces
    of scandal
Fresh from " The World." There is scarcely a
    subject he does not discourse on
Saving the question if Mary of Scotland was
    justly beheaded.
Just at the end he remembers, and states his
    opinion that Mary,
Being a beautiful lady, most likely look'd best
    with her head on ;
And that her loss must have been very great if
    she furnish'd her rooms well,
Kept blue china and paper suggestive of Morris
    and high art ;
For that in every age the Beautiful means the
    Essential.
Time presses on, and I cannot relate how a
    Brutal Athlete
Pour'd forth his scorn in a few short words on
    the luckless offender
Who had presumed to know things that weren't
    about cricket and football,
Or about trials, collections, and Midsummer
    examinations.

How he objected entirely to any nonsensical
    question

Taking us back to a time when cricket wasn't
    invented ;

Thought on the whole it was very hard luck to
    decapitate Mary ;

Thought, however, that " good Queen Bess " was
    an excellent woman.

Then spake several more : there was one in
    particular noted

For his decided opinions, and being a " practical
    man, sir ;"

Also for slow understanding and wondrous
    pragmatical manner.

Nothing on earth could excuse—he repeated it
    over and over—

Mary for breaking the LAW, or her rival for
    breaking COMMANDMENTS.

What he referr'd to he didn't explain, but he
    voted for Mary.

Laws, he said, were human ; it was not so with
    Commandments.

Last on the list was a speaker deserving of
    ampler reporting :—

" Gentlemen, that is to say Mr. President, if
    you'll excuse me,

That is allow me, I wish—I do not wish to detain
 you,
But there is one—I mean one point has escaped
the attention,
Not been mention'd by previous speakers ;" and
so on, until we
Found ourselves lost in the mazes involving this
one little point which
I have not found to this day nor ever can hope
to discover.
Poor little point that was baited and badger'd
and never o'ertaken
Till out of breath, and fatigued, and blushing,
and conscious of failure,
Down sat the speaker abruptly in midst of a
limb of a sentence.
He that had studied his "point which others had
fail'd to discover,"
Studied his one little point to such a degree of
perfection
That when it came to the birth it had died of
old age, and appear'd not.
Then the opener made a reply: he would like
to have answer'd
Arguments brought against him, but hadn't
found any to answer,

C

Hadn't observed such a thing in so many and
  eloquent speeches.
This device is certain to bring down the house—
  it's so clever ;
Likewise it saves you the trouble of finding an
  answer when needed.
Try it again and again, you're sure of your
  hearers' approval ;
Sarcasm always goes down in a house debating
  society.
When he had finish'd, the President rose to sum
  the debate up :
This is another custom of house debating so-
  cieties ;
Partly because the debates are apt to be none of
  the roughest ;
Partly because the house exists very frequently
  solely
So as to furnish a field for some embryo states-
  man or other,
Who, being chosen as president, wanting his
  weekly oration,
Chooses the method described, and appears to
  the greatest advantage.
Well then the president rose, and scatter'd good
  wishes around him

For the house he address'd, and all its connexions
and members.
Then he remarked that the speeches had all been
excessively good ones ;
Own'd it was perfectly true that there *were* two
sides to the question ;
That he himself was rejoiced that it wasn't his
duty to settle
What were his views or how he should vote ; and
being unable
To detect any flaw in a single speech or in any
Argument which they had heard, and which
might have required refutation,
Making a passing allusion to time and the swift-
ness thereof, he
Call'd upon those who believed that Mary was
justly beheaded
Straightway to hold up their hands, whereby it
was shown that opinion
Sided with Mary, which proved that axiom of
Eton debating,
(Which may be likewise discover'd in our repre-
sentative chamber)   [of party,
If the question discuss'd can be made a question
Most of the speakers are Whig, and most of the
voters are Tory.

THE TALE OF A TOP.

Being a Moral Story, wherein is exemplified the Reward of Virtue.

CONFOUND all saints and saintliness, say I! A sentiment which, after mature experience, I have come most entirely to rely on and adopt. What on earth (or above the earth, as far as I can see) induces people to be such fools I can't conceive. But the incontestable fact remains— People are such fools. I suppose the species is necessary to the economy of nature : it certainly is to the maintenance of knaves. And unless they make themselves useful to their superiors, their mission on earth is unaccomplished ; the reverse being equally true. This is a truth I have ever borne in mind, and as long as I live will never forget. For myself I always did hate saintliness, and my familiarity with all its extreme follies, as exemplified in my brother Jim, has added to my dislike an intensified contempt. For if ever there did live a fool for the sole purpose of benefiting his neighbours it was Jim. He was only two years younger than I was, but from the time that he first began to walk he was my fulsome admirer and slave. My father used feebly to object; my mother to praise Jim's "patience" and "sweetness of disposition;" qualities, as I pointed out to her, which he shared with those noble animals the ass and the sheep. At which she smiled and was satisfied.

I remember we used to devote our spare time to the intellectual amusement of spinning tops of our own manufacture, and seeing whose could stay up the longest. Mine always did. I think Jim knew that if he didn't he would repent it. But when my sister Mary joined in, hers used to beat both of ours. She laughed at that, but I couldn't stand it, and boxed her ears, which Jim accordingly kissed, like the pious brother in the story books. Mary was an "invalid," as they called it, and lay in bed all the morning, cutting tops generally. There was one top she made (the hero of my story) which beat all the others. Whirligig she called it. She was awfully fond of it; and so was I; but when I took it from her, my father made such a row about "robbing an invalid," and suchlike rant, that for the sake of a quiet life I didn't try it again, openly, at least. But when Mary grew worse and worse and could hardly lift her hand from her side, she still kept the top—the dog in the manger—and when she was too bad to hold it, she used to call Jim, and make him perform, but would never allow me to touch it. So one day when she was asleep, and every one else was out, I stole it from under her pillow, to serve her out, and hid it in a drawer. But she made up such a disturbance, that the whole household made a grand search, and found it. At last she died, "commending," with her very "last breath," to the "dutiful care" of the darling Jim the precious Whirligig, which, with plenteous outpouring of tears, he accepted; swearing to keep it as long as he lived. And so the little beast got the top to himself. But the end was different.

That same winter the tables were most satis-factorily turned. Father went out fishing one terribly cold day up into the hills, where he often used to go for the same purpose, usually with Jim. But he happened to leave him behind that day, to stay with my mother, who had been ill since Mary expired. So father went out alone, not telling us where he was going. That night he did not come home to dinner; and as he was usually punctual for meals, my mother chose to be anxious on the subject, and to wait dinner, in spite of all I could say. So at last I went down and had mine alone; and very jolly it was, too—so jolly, that I wished father would always be late for dinner, and mother too anxious to go down. Somehow or other I fell asleep after I had done, and when I woke up it was quite late. Running up to bed, I met my mother. "Your father has not come home yet. Where's Jim; do you know?" "No; nor care." For I hated Jim by that time. "Won't you ask the servants if they've seen him?" But I was really much too sleepy, and so went straight up to bed. Before long I was awakened by a horrid noise below. I jumped up and dressed to find out what it was about. All the dalesmen were in the hall, talking their vile dialect like a congress of garrulous polar bears. It seemed that neither father nor Jim had come back, and these worthies had been called to assist in the search. For although there was no snow, it was the hardest frost I had ever known in the moun-

tains.   Hence the excitement.   Father used
often to go and fish in a tarn up in the hills,
about three miles from the house ; and there we
determined to look for them.   It was a queer
place.   On three sides the rocks went sheer
down into the water ; and from these rocks we
used to fish ; and, sure enough, when we got in
sight, I saw through my glasses two figures sitting on a ledge some fifty feet above the surface.
I told the huntsman, who was walking ahead.
He wanted the glasses, but the clumsy brute
would have been sure to break them, so I told
him to shout at father, instead.   But no
answer was returned, except by the echo, which
was wonderfully clear and loud.   I did curse
pretty well.   It was really too bad of father to
make us come after him all this way and then
not answer us.   I wanted the men to turn back,
but they wouldn't.   We scrambled round the
tarn, shouting as we went along, but no answer.
At last, when we got near enough, I threw a
stone.   I thought he must answer that, but,
though it was a good shot, he never moved.
That oaf of a huntsman turned round and swore
at me, but it was a way he had, and I never

cared for him. We came nearer. Father was sitting with his back propped up on a large rock, with the rod in his hands, and Jim seemed lying asleep with his head in his lap. He was always fond of striking attitudes, the little fool. But when the huntsman climbed up to them I heard him shout out (I was some way behind), and saw him fall forward on his hands and knees. So I hurried up to see what was the matter. I was never so frightened in my life, as when one of the men took me up to the place, and I saw father with his hands and face quite blue, and his eyes shut, still clutching the rod ; and Jim's coat over his neck. Jim's head had fallen into father's lap, and his face was cold and blue also. The huntsman was blubbering like a great baby, as he said, " Your father must have fallen asleep from the cold. Master Jim's gone out alone at dead of night to find him frozen. He's tried to chafe his hands, and taken off his own coat to warm a dead man into life " (that was just like Jim), "and has fallen asleep himself." Every one began to blubber thereupon, except me. I never would make a baby of myself. The men carried the bodies down the hill home. But I stayed behind, for I knew what an awful row there would be in the house, and there I saw Jim's coat lying on the rocks, for they had forgotten it. I lifted it up, and in the breast pocket I found Whirligig, safe and sound. You may be sure I took precious care of it down from the tarn; and it was lucky I did, for afterwards, just before the funeral, mother asked me, "where Mary's top was; he always said he would have it put in his coffin." But it never was, as you may think. And I have Whirligig to this day. And so *I* got the top in the end.

SONG OF LIBERTY.

THERE is a sound in our ears,
   Swung down by the bells of time;
It comes as a sound of tears,
   In vague and ineffable rhyme.

It calls the Creator's creation :
   " Up, ye down-trodden, arise !
Now lives the free god of your nation,
   Now smitten credulity dies !

Come forth from the gloom of the gloaming,
  In which you have passionless run,
And quit you the shroud of your moaning,
  In the light of the life-giving sun.

The kingdom of ages that were
  To the kingdom of ages to come :
Shut your ears to the curse of Despair,
  List to virginal Liberty's hum.

The mantle of freedom when fallen
  Was not left at the place where it fell ;
Break the bond of your bonds then, ye callen
  Of centuries, bear yourselves well !

The God of your fathers he calls you
  To take up the tale of your birth ;
Then what of oppression that palls you ?
  'Tis but earthborn, give earth back to earth ! "

It is gone with the boom of its booming,
  It is swept on, that voice of the bells ;
In the dawn where the future is looming
  Still with time-swollen cadence it swells.

A ROMANCE.

"And they have likewise an infernal machine, whereby a heavy weight, being cunningly balanced on a slightly-opened door, shall suddenly and supernally descend on the head of the unwitting victim who attempteth the opening of the same."—*History of the Ancient Britons.*

HAST ever seen an idle boy
Designing to disgust, annoy,
Foil, and if possible destroy
Some youth whose anguish is *his* joy,
In very wantonness employ
That engine, instrument or toy,
    The Booby-trap.

Hast ever seen the fiendish grin,
With which that little imp of sin
Will almost leap out of his skin
To see his victim enter in,—
(The victim is by no means thin,
Less valorous than a Paladin,
More learned than a Capuchin),
Beneath that unsuspected gin
    The Booby-trap.

A piece of string, a little care,
A heavy lexicon, a pair

Of boots, a steady hand, some fair
Spring water in an earthenware
And not too costly vessel :—there
You have that pit-fall, springe, or snare,
     The Booby-trap.

This weapon balanced on the door,
We wait outside (an hour or more
If necessary), till the floor
Creaks with the victim's weight : a score
Of seconds is reduced to four !
And four to one ! ! and all is o'er ! ! !
 * * * * *
Quite calmly, though immersed in gore,
The victim murmurs, " What a bore !
     A Booby-trap !"

THE REASON WHY.

June, 1875.

AT the magic words, " And now,"
 Runs a tremor through the hall.
Joy awakes on every brow,
 Sleep is cast away from all ;

And the crowd with heads erect,
  Wake like birds by sunbeams kiss'd.
And this is why a certain sect
  Is sometimes termed " Revivalist."

NAMELESS.

THE voice of the forest is swelling
  Creation's whisper'd praise ;
The freshness of love is dwelling
  In the life-giving sunshine rays.

But the breeze o'er the upland sweeping
  Is sad, as it kisses the linn,
For the streamlet's waves are weeping
  Mid the rapid's hurrying din.

For the chill cold corpse in the river
  No sympathy, sorrow, or care,
Though the parting must be for ever,
  No succouring hand is there.

The folly of man hath an ending
  With its vision of vain delight,
But her spirit its way is wending
  Through the crystal fields of light.

In the fair blue dome of heaven
'Mid the radiant spheres on high,
To her soul is fresh knowledge given,
The solution of How and Why.

But the corpse in the current is whirling,
Coffinless, cold, and fair,
And the hungry ripple is curling
Round the matted and tangled hair.

And the breeze of the forest laden
With the sigh of the coming storm,
Sings the dirge of the drownèd maiden,
As it sweeps o'er her pallid form.

NOVACASTELLANA.

(Appeared in the *Etonian.*)

Being the Diary of a Week's " Sapping" for the " Newcastle Scholarship," March, 1876.

MONDAY.—I came to the conclusion that I was born to do great things; thought I was probably cut out for a poet; wasn't quite sure,

however, as I didn't know much about poetry or
poet, except that the one has rhymes, the other
long hair. *Happy thought.* Write something
good for *The Etonian,* and sign my name at the
bottom.

After 10.—Went to " Mathematics," tried to
evolve the plot of my poem, to be called " The
Fourth of June;" only succeeded in evolving
fifty lines for inattention. *Mem.—* Evident want
of sympathy between mathematical and poetical
minds. Produced a stanza during 11 o'clock
school :—

> " Behold the Fourth of June
>   Comes with a merry tune,
>   And with the joyful noise
>   Of many happy boys."

After 12.—Spent half an hour in reading over
my production ; thought it very good. Fagged
a Lower Boy to suggest rhymes, wanted a rhyme
to "dawn," he could only suggest "yawn,"
which wouldn't do. Finally came to the conclusion that poeticising wasn't in my line. I
then went to see my tutor, who said I had
better go in for the Newcastle. Wasted the rest
of " after 12 " in thinking how I should set to

work : decided at last to get up all the "tips," and to cram everything that would pay. *Happy thought,* to publish a book of " Newcastle tips " some day.

After 4.—Went "down town," and ordered Jowett's "Plato," Donaldson's "Pindar," Shilleto's "Thucydides," and six grammars, including Madvig and Goodwin. Just before school saw my books arrive in a wheelbarrow. I began to have qualms.

After tea.—Unpacked my new possessions ; didn't know which to begin with ; finally fell asleep over the first chapter of Goodwin, and was late for prayers. Went to bed early, dreamt Professors Goodwin and Madvig were quarrelling over the relative value of their particles. M. had rather the best of it.

TUESDAY.—In the morning Smith (a fellow-student) came into my room, for the purpose, as he said, of putting me up to some good "tips," of which, of course, I must be profoundly ignorant. His first question was, "By what Latin authors is reference made to Johannes Gilpinus ?" I rose to the occasion, and promptly referred him to Horace, Ode 1, Book III.

"Post equitem sedet atra cura." He looked
queer, but persevered, maintaining that the
Romans had a Four-in-Hand Club and a Rotten
Row. This I emphatically denied, but he, with
exultation blazing from every feature of his
countenance, pulled a Virgil out of his pocket, and,
pointing to Georgic III. 106, exclaimed, "There!
Read that!" I obeyed and read,—

> "Illi instant verbere torto
> Et proni dant lora ; volat vi fervidus axis.
> Nec mora nec requies ; at fulvæ nimbus arenæ
> Tollitur."

This was rather a crusher, but I bided my time,
and on his asking who was the most unctuous of
the Greeks, I snatched up the now welcome
Virgil, and, disdaining such small fry as the
Georgics, turned to Æneid I., where at the 41st
line I triumphantly read, "Ajacis oilei." He
retired crestfallen ; I took a little necessary
refreshment.

After 2.—Looked in White's "Junior Student's
English-Latin Dictionary," for the Latin equiva-
lents to *idiosyncrasy, snob, water-on-the-brain,
gingham,* and *syntax.* Couldn't find them, and
became disconsolate. *Syntax* especially puzzled

me ; nothing could be simpler than the natural rendering " *Peccati vectigal,*" but how to account for the *y* instead of the *i* in the English ? Would the Newcastle Examiners ask the question ? I fervently hoped not, and went to *present* myself at *absence* (remember this as a capital instance of Euripidical *oxymoron*).

After 4.—Took a little exercise with the Beagles, and trod eleven times on the tails of the hounds. In the evening, being in want of stimulants to brace me up for an hour or two's hard work, read the *Police News* and *The Etonian,* and was thus enabled to devote my entire attention to study. Found that 1876 is an *Annus Bissextus* (does that mean that it is *bisected?*), that a naval *action* was fought at *Actium* (tautology,) some time B.C. or A.D., and that an Iambic is the same thing as a Tragic Senarius. Went to bed at 11. *Mem.*—Hard day's work.

WEDNESDAY.—Very tired ; late for school.

After 12.—Intended to read Aristophanes ; went to the School Library, as I had heard of an edition there in which some one had marked all the " tips ;" found it was out. Went to Tom Brown's and spent an hour and a half in choosing a pair of trousers; couldn't decide between a green and red Angola and a pale salmon Chesterfield.

After 4.—Read thirty lines of Jowett's "Plato," thought it rather foolish; tried a Greek play, but couldn't find any "tips."

After 6.—Very cross and miserable. Sat up till 2, and read chapters of Thucydides and Herodotus alternately, to get accustomed to the style of both authors. Went to bed with a headache and wet handkerchief tied round my head. Dreamt I was Newcastle Scholar, crowned with laurel; woke up and found the laurel was only the handkerchief.

THURSDAY.—Late again for early school. Got 100 lines, which I made my fag write out instead of having his breakfast.

After 12.—Thought I would study a little Latin; got out pen, ink, and paper. N.B.— Persius evidently wrote of me when he said, Sat. III. 12—15,—

> " Tunc queritur, crassus calamo quod pendeat humor,
> Nigra quod infusa vanescat sepia lympha,
> Dilutas queritur geminet quod fistula guttas."

For I could not get my pen to write properly;

finally gave it up as a bad job, and took to a
pencil, with which I dotted down notes as I
skimmed through book after book of classical
lore. Horace struck me as being an inordinate
wine-bibber, withal somewhat chary of providing
a bottle at his own table ; witness the 20th ode
of the first book (I had "Smart" by my side,
or I should not have found that out). As for
Virgil's Æneids, the earlier ones seemed to be a
prolix panegyric on the piety of " Pius Æneas,"
the last four nothing more or less than a care-
fully-compiled obituary. Query : Is not Bohn
more worthy of our admiration than either
Flaccus or Maro ?

After 4.—Eschewed *Beagles* and *Fives* (why
not *Fours?* I defy any one to answer that),
and again sat me down with the utmost resigna-
tion at my hated *bureau.* After an hour's unin-
terrupted cogitation, resolved to look up a few
hints for Latin verse and prose. To begin with, I
quite agreed with Tennyson in stigmatizing the
former as a—

    " Barbarous experiment, barbarous hexameters,"

but as the Newcastle Examiners would, in spite

of the Laureate's openly expressed opinion, be
sure to set a passage for translation, and as I
was bent on being, if not Scholar, at any rate
Medallist, and yet no Medallist (you know, of
course, that no medal is given now-a-days. For
the construction, see Euripides' Hecuba, 610).
I thought I would note down some likely
morceaux to take into the examination on my
shirt-sleeve. I. Suitable terminations to Penta-
meters—" Talia verba refert," " Candida gutta
nivis" (Snowdrop), " Marmora clara maris."
II. *Proper* names " *Oppianicus ;*" but might not
the examiners call that a false quantity? Or,
still better, " *Herzegovina ;*" but alas! on second
thoughts I remember having heard the other
day that in that word also, the *i* is short. Thus
baffled, I gave up versifying in disgust.

After tea.—Tried a little Latin prose, and
read through Livy, Cicero, and Tacitus. Be-
coming considerably fuddled with the mixture,
I turned, in order to clear my head, to the
" Latin Primer," which I had always heard of
as a model of innocence contrasted with the
duplicity of Madvig. However, I got so confused by the money-table on page 130, where

mention is made of no other animals than *asses*, and *asses usuræ* (as if a female ass could be a *usurer*), that I threw the book down in despair and went to bed.

FRIDAY might almost be called a "blank" day as regards Newcastle work, for after 12 I had to do my verses which I had shirked, fondly hoping that I should escape detection. My tutor, however, had apparently kept his weather eye open, for to my unutterable dismay he gently hinted to me at 12 o'clock that "Gradus ad Parnassum" would constitute an agreeable form of amusement for my leisure hours, until I had shown him up the sum of 30 Ele-giacs (vide Paley's Note on Æschylus' Agamemnon, 671). Miserable things! Why is the rising generation obliged to display its strong (?) classical propensities in the development of so paltry an effort?

" Tempora mutantur, nos et mutamur in illis."

What would Ovid say, were he to see me sulkily scribbling hackneyed imitations of his impassioned Muse?

After 2.—Showed up my verses and tried a little work. Began by studying Latin and Greek numerals; got as far as 7, where I stopped. Why were there 7 Sages of Greece; 7 Kings of Rome; 7 Wonders of the World; 7 Champions of Christendom; finally, why are there 7 days of the week? Asked Smith, but he couldn't tell me.

After 4.—Played my House Fives Sweep-stakes, First Ties. Was beaten at "love" each game. For the first time I forgot myself and volubly anathematized the devoted "Newcastle," as the cause of my ill-luck.

After tea.—Took up a Homer and read in the 19th Odyssey an account of pig-sticking as carried on in those days by Ulysses. Compare this with the Prince of Wales' recent exploits in India. Looking through a Roman History, I was sorry to find that Cæsar made use of bad language, "*Et tu brute.*" I am ashamed to say that I followed his example, vituperating the Scholarship in the very same words. Was I wrong?

SATURDAY.—Came to the conclusion that a little light work would be advisable after my exertions of the last few days. Began by turning my thoughts to the Divinity Papers, on which I had heard great stress is laid by the examiners. I was a little puzzled at starting by the word *patriarch.* Does it answer to the modern *patriot?* I next tried to institute a comparison between the 1st Book of Chronicles and the " Eton College Chronicle," but failed. Found also that Jezebel was a *Sid-onian*, but thought it wouldn't do to contrast that with the *Et-onian.* Happy thought! I suddenly recollected that I had seen it mentioned in that veracious print the *World*, a month ago, that the Old Testament was written with 5642 words (remember, mum's the word for that ; the examiners, if they are men of the *world*, are bound to ask it).

After 4.—Broached the Acts (does that signify the doings, or is it merely an abbreviation for the *accounts* of the Apostles ?) with Wordsworth, Humphrey, Alford, and Bloomfield at my side (I mean their commentaries, not the reverend gentlemen themselves), but came to grief over Wordsworth's lengthy *objections* and *replies* in his preface to the seventh chapter. Gave up the whole thing in disgust ; determined to " bar " the *New*castle as a *nui*sance ; sent all my books indiscriminately, grammars, cribs, commentaries,

down town to Hetherington's, to be sold at the
next auction there; ate, or rather drank, my tea
with a lightened heart and infinite gusto, and
went to bed as happy as a king.

BALLAD.

" 'TIS three months syne, O three months syne,
    Three weary months to me,
Since last I saw the glint on the sails
    Sink down beneath the sea.

"O weel, weel may the good ship glide
    Across the stormy main ;
But, sair, oh sair, my heart misgives—
    They never will come again.

" The storm-blast whistles o'er the roof,
    And down the narrow lane,
And every blast screams out to me—
    ' They never will come again.'

" The storm-clouds scurry past the sky,
  And fierce they frown on me :
They have seen the good ship stagger and sink
  Beneath a foaming sea."

The widow rose and shut the Book,
  Wet with the tears she sheds,
And cast one long and lingering look
  On those three empty beds ;

And then she lifts the broken latch—
  Flings open the rattling door ;
In her eyes is the glint of the flashing foam—
  In her ears the dull sea's roar.

There stood three figures by her side,
  White through the murky air ;
And the rain did not moisten their long thin
    hands,
  And the wind did not stir their hair.

" My sons, my sons, my own dear sons,
  In truth are ye come to me ?
Or cannot your troubled spirits rest
  In the deeps of the troubled sea ?"

And then came a voice like a silver lute
  Through the deep bass roar of the wind,
And fear, like a shadow, went before,
  But a sweet peace came behind.

" Oh dinna' ye weep for us, mother,
  For vain the tears ye shed,
And sweet is the sleep we sleep, mother,
  For in heaven is made our bed.

" Around our bodies the corals bloom,
  And above them the deep sea rolls ;
But little we reck of our foul bodies—
  Thy prayers have saved our souls."

THE QUEEN.

March, 1876.

THEY may talk of their " Empress " and titles of
    fame,
  High sounding whatever they be ;
They may say what they will, but I love the old
    name,
  The Queen of Old England for me !

That name will stand out as the brightest and
    best
    In the tale of the brave and the free,
And it still strikes a chord in each Englishman's
    breast,
    Oh ! the Queen of old England for me !

When through treachery Emperors climb to a
    throne,
    Their baseness with horror we see,
And proudly we turn to the Queen of our own ;
    Oh! the Queen of old England for me!

Yes, I love the old name for it speaks to my
    heart,
    Where'er the inscription I see,
And to new-fangled titles I'm loth to depart,
    Oh ! the Queen of old England for me !

What mean these devices I cannot divine
    (In spite of the words I've been told)
While snobs and while toadies their efforts com-
    bine
    In a project to " gild the fine gold."

Well! well!   After all it don't matter one bit
  How at last on this point they agree,
Though they call her what names to themselves
    may seem fit,
  Still she's Queen of old England for me!

———————

SUMMER THOUGHTS.

'Tis the happy time when summer
  Sock-cads delicacies hawk,
And I hear the Eton drummer
  Practising in Poet's Walk ;

Then my playful fancies wander
  Till my pictures seem a blur,
While abstractedly I ponder
  On the fact that mortals err.

Some there are to whom a wicket
  Seems the best of things on earth,
(Thus reflected I on cricket,
  Part in anger, part in mirth,)

Others prizes love more dearly
  Far than gold or precious gems ;
Not a few spend very nearly
  Half their life upon the Thames.

Some take exercise in walking,
  Some delight in food and tea,
Some waste all their time in talking,
  And the rest in thought like me.

Others will discourse severely,
  Meaning nothing all the time,
Telling you that life is merely
  What I cannot say in rhyme.

Much by careful calculations
  Out of nothing can be got,
Indeterminate equations,
  Things that tell you what is what

Or what isn't. Which is grander,
  To become a living oar,
Or through nothing to meander,
  Seeking nothing evermore ?

This I leave to coming ages
To unravel ; this may be
Food for undeveloped sages
Of the future, not for me.

"QUIPPE TER ET QUATER."

THREE OR FOUR QUIPS.

Virgil. Georgic I. 161. " Nec surgere messes."
—Why not " Nec strawberry messes ? "

Virgil. Georgic I. 163. "Tarda volventia plaus-
tra."—London "Growler."

Virgil. Georgic I. 229. " Bootes."—Hotel func-
tionary.

Virgil. Æneid. I. 69. " Submersas obrue pup-
pes."—Precedent for the ordinary method of
disposing of young dogs.

PROMETHEUS VINCTUS.

ABOVE, all round, and far below,
Lie dazzling sheets of purest snow ;

So pure that nought is like it, but the white
Of fleecy clouds that lie in azure light.
All snow, all snow, save where the mountain reft
Displays adown its side a hideous cleft.
Silence around, no life, all cold and dead,
Never in that rare air do mortal footsteps tread

Only from that chasm can be heard the roar,
Where the hidden waters never-ending pour ;
Only from the steep side of the mountain tall
Can be heard the echoes of the avalanche fall ;
Only in the tempests, when the lightnings flash,
Can be heard amidst the rocks the awful thunder crash.

Surely these the fragments are of that enormous tower,
Form'd by Titans in old time to seize the heavenly power ;
When the earth resounded with their battle-cry,
And re-echoing sent it pealing to the sky,
Sterner still and sterner raged their conflict wild,
Higher still and higher they the mountains piled ;

E

Louder than all thunder crash'd their mighty fall,
Filling the whole firmament to heaven's highest
	hall ;
When the great Olympian conquer'd them at
	last,
And bound them deep beneath the earth in iron
	fetters fast.

Long ago Prometheus told them nought but
	cunning skill
Would gain for them high heaven, and foil the
	Thunderer's will,
But they would not listen, that old giant brood
Thought that force would conquer, rough, and
	strong, and rude ;
Now they lie for ever all bound in caverns low,
And Prometheus on the rock lies, doom'd to
	tortures slow.

All creation mourns him, all the hills and vales,
From the fountains of the streams rise many
	bubbling wails,
And the untamed beasts of the forest lament
	with many a groan ;
And the living things of Nature together for him
	moan,

And the numberless laugh of the ocean was
    hush'd for a while at his fate,
And the birds of the woodlands for him each
    one complain'd with his mate.

All creation mourn'd him—the great foreseeing
    mind ;
All creation mourn'd him—first lover of mankind ;
All creation mourn'd him—him, from heaven
    who stole
The pure bright flame for mankind, fit emblem
    of his soul ;
Dauntless Zeus-defying, ever 'midst his pain
Waiting still for better things and a new and
    better reign,
Waiting till the cycling years bring back the age
    of gold,
And still remembering 'midst his woes the time
    of Saturn old.

There in that black chasm, with the snow around,
Suffering endless torture in iron fetters bound,
On that rock he lieth, godlike, still, and great,
Waiting the deliverer who comes to end his fate :

All around the mountains evermore shall stand,
Watching still their prisoner great, like sentries
   in the land.

MY NOVEL.

A is the gallant
   In doublet and hose,
With a sword and a swagger
   And aquiline nose.
B is the maiden
   In purple and buff,
With a hat like a steeple,
   And oh ! such a ruff.

A loves the maiden
   So gentle and slim :
The maiden, moreover,
   Is partial to him.
But C (that's the villain),
   Dread foeman of A,
Is averse to the union—
   So opens the play.

C tells the maiden's mother,
  And the maiden's father too,
" Such irregular proceedings
  Will really never do :
That your daughter, that your darling,
  That the ' pearl ' so dearly prized—
With a veritable beggar
  Should thus be 'compromised,'—
With a fool whose borrow'd pocket
  Was not weighted with a sou ;
Such irregular proceedings
  Would surely never do."

Up starts the angry father—
  The match had fired the train—
And I much regret to say it,
  Was disgracefully profane.
But the climax of my story
  When my talent's at my best,
And the swearing, and the cursing,
  And the breathless interest,
Came, when rushing through the garden—
  Half mad with rage and hate—
He finds that guilty couple
  In a loving *tête-à-tête*.

So A most ignobly
   Was kick'd out of doors,
And not many years after
   Fell, fighting the Moors.
B shut up in the castle,
   With never a friend,
Soon dies broken-hearted—
   And that is the end.

So this is my novel,
   Believe me it's true,
And though often repeated,
   Yet ever is new ;
For, barring the doublet,
   The hanger, and ruff,
To find similar cases
   Is easy enough.

"HODZSON."

" Thou ever strong upon the stronger side."
King John, Act iii. sc. 1.

I DON'T know whether my friend Hodzson is acquainted with the above passage; as "King John"

has not lately been set for holiday task I should
say probably not: but if he were, I think he
would say Constance paid Austria a remarkably
handsome compliment. Strong upon the stronger
side? Really, and why not? Strength is good,
a worthy desideratum, and where can it be obtained so readily as where it abounds—on the
stronger side? where be so effectual as where
best supported—by the stronger side? And I
suppose his principles are as correct as his
practice—and I never knew any one make fewer
mistakes. " Medio tutissimus ibis : " there must
be something divine about this middle-way, this
superb abstinence from the 'falsehood of ex-
tremes.' To be enthusiastic — so is 'Arry
Snooks on his summer trip to Wales: to be
stern, cynical, contemptuous,—that is but a com-
mon symptom of indigestion. But to be Hodzson, invariably to be swayed by calm prudence,
by practical common-sense, by a supreme, im-
maculate and universal indifference—that is an
ideal not easily realized.

Not long ago, under the cruel necessity of
Sunday Questions, my attention was occupied
by the founders of Jesuitism ; and being re-

quired to account for their personal influence, I
informed my division master (not in my own
words) that I believed it was from the force of
their " intense, enthusiastic, and unselfish belief."
And I hope that the circumstances being considered, my fraud may be accounted pious. Un-
professionally I can't believe that to have been
the case.   Why, just look at Hodzson as he sits
at the end of the table.   There sits Influence in-
carnate : I cannot describe him, you see, with
Anglo-Saxon words or without a capital letter.
Do you see Smith's anxious gaze Hodzson-
wards as he makes that little joke of his, his
joke redolent of midnight oil ?   Poor Smith ! it
is made under approval, and who will laugh,
" Jove non probante " ?   And there is Jones
holding forth with timid profoundness about our
next subject for debate.   He has considered the
subject as usual profoundly, so he says—Hodzson
thinks profoundly about nothing—why should
he ? But, a word, and down goes Jones's theory;
contemptuous silence, and the eloquent philosopher's appetite is spoiled.   Look at any one
telling a story, a private anecdote confided to
his neighbour.   Isn't the corner of the narrator's

eye expressive? Do you see who is sought out
and found? Is it to Robinson alone that Brown
tells that exceedingly interesting anecdote about
Heavy's crab? Faith? Enthusiasm? On Sunday mornings we are not unfrequently assured
that our Eton is a little world, that what is true
of the greater is true also of the less. And if so,
I could controvert by the fact the author of
Ecclesiastical Biographies. There sits the con-
futation. Can power be more absolute? And I
never heard of Hodzson indulging in enthusiasm
or superabundant faith. Nor is it virtue or
talent or even physical excellence that constitutes his power. It is nothing remarkable.
It is rather the absence of anything remarkable.
Friend Hodzson is not clever: neither is he
stupid: in games he is neither good nor bad;
in work he is by no means distinguished, but
then he is not more than usually ignorant. He
is neither so high as to be too admirable for
familiarity nor so low as to be simply despicable.
He is always in all things on the standpoint.
Hark at Jones appealing to first principles. " Jus-
tice—struggling nobly into civilization—eternal
laws—unspeakable Turk," I can hear every now

and then from my end of the table. "Very
well, but practically,—" says Hodzson. Did you
ever see any one more completely quelled? "Practically." To carry Hodzson away with you into
the seventh heaven! My dear foolish Jones, I think
you had better go and finish those verses. And
now that Jones has gone, listen : "Confound it,
you know, to settle the Eastern Question by an
appeal to first principles!" says Hodzson the
sensible. We admire, and sympathize, and are
satisfied. But Robinson is telling his story.
When he came in half an hour late for school he
had dropped his extra work in the mud, and had
to go back to copy it over again. I laugh, a very
good excuse that. But, "You shouldn't tell so
many, your lies are quite stale by now," says
Hodzson the virtuous. How admirable is virtue! Confound those risible muscles of mine!
And when Robinson retires to meet that en-
gagement we are informed that friend R. is a
disgrace to the house. And again we admire
and wonder and agree. "Strong upon the
stronger side"—was ever any one more so?
Yet it sounds easy enough to come to the vic-
tor's rescue and be remarkable for nothing. But

every one can't see which is the stronger, exactly
hit off the one tone sure to meet with approval
because it is the average tone. Can you, for instance, brave the great Griffin, and brave him
successfully because you see where public
opinion will support you? Griffin large of body,
mighty in mind, before whose force and readi-
ness we all hang our diminished heads? He is
talking now, more fluent and amusing and para-
doxical than usual. Look how Hodzson listens
critically with head on one side, six inches below
Griffin's. " That is very amusing, and it is very
kind of you to put yourself to such trouble for
my amusement "; one hears it in his laugh. Not
even Griffin can make an impression, can make
him forget who is the stronger. You will hear
as soon as he goes how absurd it is to talk like
that. And we all agree : how should we not ?
he is the spokesman of our thoughts, and therein
lies the secret of his power. The common-sense
of humanity, it is an expression often enough in
our mouths, but who knows it, who sees it clearly,
who invariably represents it ? One is too extravagant, another pitched too low. But here is a
true representative of public opinion, an infalli-

ble popularity gauge, a personified average. Sucking-philosopher Jones may convert us by a happy flight of eloquence; Robinson pervert us by a decrease of vulgarity and an increase of wit, but it is only Hodzson who neither converts nor perverts, but simply and solely represents. I should think the species has always existed, has constantly plodded through life with this consistent absence of unnecessary emotion, with a mind clever enough to understand a few commonplaces, to take a fairly intelligent view of every-day matters, stupid enough to be obdurate to all persuasion, and take its own small powers of comprehension as a universal test of truth,— preceding not guiding, led but seeming to lead, uniform, callous, and self-sufficient. I believe there is in this neighbourhood a tombstone erected to the memory of Sarah Jenkins, "an amiable daughter, a conscientious wife, and a judicious grandmother. Her distinguishing characteristic was propriety." I have not heard that the Hodzsons intermarried with the Jenkinses, but if it had been so, it would have been a striking example of the fact that character is transmitted by race. But I suppose the world has never lacked the like. I can fancy, to recur to the age of blue paint, the radical reformer of the times rising in full assembly with a specimen of the " bracæ " for which the Romans subsequently admired our ancestors. He would suggest that the present costume was not ornamental, neither was it useful. It certainly was not decent. Here is that which will satisfy all wants. But to him uprises the sage, chosen spokesman of contemporary folly. " Reform certainly was right, in moderation. He would improve, not abolish, the customs of his ancestors. He need not oppose the absurd motion suggested, but would rather propose an amendment." And forthwith, I have no doubt, he would lay on the table a proposal for reforming the popular costume by the tasteful addition of yellow stripes. Certainly, in life, as well as in arguments, ignorance and indifference, are great advantages ; but I think they are sometimes abused.

EXCELSIOR.

" The floods are in all the lower rooms, and we hear of a man taking his pig with him, as an inmate of the upper story.—*The Times*, November, 1875.

THE floods were coming upstairs fast,
As by the first-floor landing pass'd
A youth who cried, while on his back
A pig was struggling in a sack,
                    Excelsior.

Its head stuck out, its beady eye
Flash'd with regret for straw and sty,
While like discordant bagpipes rung
The accents of its well-known tongue,
                    Excelsior.

" This floor will do," the old man said,
" Try not the attics overhead,
The stairs are straight, the sack is wide,"
And loud a grunt within replied,
                    Excelsior.

" Oh, stay," the maiden said, " and rest
That wrinkled snout upon this breast."
The porker scorns the soft appeal,
And still keeps up the ceaseless squeal,
                    Excelsior.

" Don't let him out !" the old man spake,
" Think of the awful rout he'll make."
This was the peasant's last good night ;
A voice cried, half-way up the flight,
          Excelsior.

The pig was drown'd ; when dawn'd the day
Lifeless but beautiful he lay,
But ere he died, from attic high
Grunted still scornful of his sty,
          Excelsior.

FRAGMENT.

K is the Kingdom he's come to reform,
E the Entrenchments of vice that he'll storm,
N the New light that will lighten our yoke ;
E the Enlighten'd Electors of Stoke :
A the great Anger that fills him with fire,
L is the Law that he'll raise from the mire :
Y 's the Yahoo to the kingdom unknown
    Till Kenealy arose, and Kenealy alone.

THE PHILOSOPHER AND THE PHILANTHROPIST.

SEARCHING an infinite Where,
Probing a bottomless When,
  Dreamfully wandering,
  Ceaselessly pondering,
What is the Wherefore of men :
Bartering life for a There,
Selling his soul for a Then,
  Baffling obscurity,
  Conning futurity,
Usefulest, wisest of men !

Grasping the Present of Life,
Seizing a definite Now,
  Labouring thornfully,
  Banishing scornfully
Doubts of his Whither and How,
Spending his substance in Strife,
Working a practical How,
  Letting obscurity
  Rest on futurity,
Usefuler, wiser, I trow.

THE CAIRN.

TELL me, thou cairn of memory old,
  The meaning that in thy semblance lies,
Dost guard the last sleep of a warrior bold,
  Who died as the war-stricken hero dies ?

Did the wild dirge swell o'er the mountain peak,
  Like the moan of the wind through the pine-
    tree wood ?
Did the sadden'd note of the clarion speak
  Of the loss of the brave, and the true, and the
    good ?

Or didst thou behold the mystic gloom
  That erst o'ershadow'd religion's shrine ?
Didst thou rise as the self-given victim's tomb ?
  Was an office of vain superstition thine ?

Didst thou a conqueror's triumph share,
  When, echoing down the rock-girt vale,
The swell of victory fill'd the air,
  " Hail to the Cambrian Chieftain, hail ?"

Thou hast heard the fitful breeze rejoice,
  Whate'er thy birth, whate'er thy lore,
Thou hast heard the wail of the storm wind's voice,
  With the thunder's roll and the torrent's roar.

F

May'st thou in cold indifference yet
   A thousand winters' fierceness brave,
For thou markest what we may ne'er forget,
   A warrior's triumph or a chieftain's grave.

CLODHOPPERS.

No, don't ask me, Joe,
   Of Tom that is pass'd away,
Just seventeen years ago ;
   Seventeen years, did I say ?
For it seems but a week, but a week since poor
   Tom pass'd away.

No, don't ask me ; he's gone.
   Brother Tom has gone to his place,
And I'm left here alone,
   Here, till I end my days.
But, Joe, in the other world, how dare I look
   Tom in the face ?

Ah, you remember, Joe,
   We were boys together at school.

I slighted him—him you know,
  I call'd him a sorry fool.
And we thought him a dolt, you remember, he
  bore it all so cool.

Do you remember, Joe,
  That day when we play'd at ball ?
And he was standing so,
  Just under the old school wall,
Standing, watching our game, as he used to, just
  within call. .

And how my ball hit a child
  That was playing near in the hay ?
And how he ran up, and smiled
  To it, just in his old kind way ?
And coax'd it, and brought it home, while we went
  on with our play.

And then that winter too,
  When I was a-courting Jane ;
And we walk'd down, I and you,
  Just to look at her house again,
And we saw him watching us there, at the corner
  of Borough Lane.

Yes, I remember now,
    Just seventeen years ago,
That day when I told him how
    I loved her, and all you know,
That he trembled, and didn't answer at first;
    you remember, Joe?

And then that wintry day
    We walk'd out, Jane and I,
And met him, Jane turn'd away,
    And I said, " Did you come to spy?"
I remember, Joe, as he turn'd, that I saw a tear
    in his eye.

And it wasn't long after, I think,
    On the ice, on the pond down there,
That we saw him again on the brink,
    And he call'd to us; Jane, my dear,
You remember we turn'd away, and pretended
    not to hear.

And then of a sudden the ice
    Gave way; with a terrible cry,
And just in front of my eyes,
    As I struggled, fit to die,
A figure leap'd down from the bank—it seem'd
    to fall from the sky.

Then o'er me a darkness came
  Like a veil, and a chilling pain,
Yet I seem'd to be all a-flame
  With horror and fear for Jane,
And I thought of Tom ; but, Joe, I never saw
  him again.

They say that he jump'd from the bank,
  And saved us ; they show'd me the place
He jump'd from, then he sank
  Through the cold.   God give me grace
To go where he is.   But then how dare I look
  him in the face ?

THE ASCENT OF SCAWFELL PIKE.

*(Being an Account of an Excursion made in the
Summer Holidays of* 1875.)

OUR great expedition of the season (by the
season I mean the autumn months) was to be the
ascent of Scawfell Pikes, or rather the highest of
the three, being the only one which has authentic
claims to the title of King of English mountains

(Emperor, I ought perhaps to say), and which, although its majesty is not particularly exalted compared with other and foreign rivals, at the same time reflects great credit on old England, whose *chef d'œuvre* in the mountain line it undoubtedly is. We had fixed a day for this undertaking, to which we were anxiously looking forward, myself more especially, as this was to be my maiden essay as a climber, and though we were not quite such tyros as to count the intervening hours and minutes, yet we were sufficiently interested to pull up our blinds the very first thing when the actual morning did arrive, and to thank Heaven that at least it was not raining. If any who read this are of Alpine celebrity, let them not laugh at my enthusiasm, but call to mind the old proverb which says, " A small spark kindles a great flame." Before beginning my story I will disclaim any reference to guide-books, in the majority of which there is nothing to my mind more monotonous than the constant repetition of statistics as to height, depth, length, breadth, and the numerous small-print quotations from our English poets, whose panegyrics on the lake and mountain scenery of

Cumberland and Westmoreland, although no doubt very delightful, are at the same time a little trite. But to return to my sheep, as the French would say, though, as I was the youngest of the party, the simile of a shepherd is hardly suitable in this case. There were nine of us, all told, and as we were quartered at some distance from the field, or, more truly, mountain of action, we were compelled to start early on a ten miles' drive to Bassenthwaite, whence we took train to Keswick. On arriving there, we strolled into the town, some of our party, of course, investing in the indigenous lead pencils, and finally, all squeezed into a small and rather dilapidated waggonette, driven by a greasy charioteer, who, by dint of guttural chucklings, interspersed with a series of chirruping sibilations, endeavoured to rouse the slumbering mettle of his scarcely responsive pair. However, we were taken at a moderate pace along the east shore of the lake, past Barrow and Lodore, catching delightful glimpses of their respective cascades, past the Bowder stone and Castle Crag, up through Borrowdaile to Seatollar. At Rosthwaite, the name given to a few houses about a

mile before Seatollar, we stopped to take up our
guide, by name Jackson, by trade a bootmaker,
but who, with the addition of a coat, hat, and
stick, was soon metamorphosed from the cobbler
into the mountaineer.   At the same place we
hired a pony to take over our clothes, which
were all compressed into one small portmanteau,
to Dungeon Gill Hotel, where we intended to
sleep the night, and of which more anon.   During
our drive we were preceded and followed by
waggonettes (apparently the only form of vehicle
known in that part of the world) filled with a
motley collection of tourists and holiday makers,
who, however, had different game in view, for to
our great relief we saw nothing of them for the
rest of the day.   At Seatollar we disembarked,
dismissed our unctuous coachman and his jaded
steeds, and commenced operations by crossing
a small bridge near the rise of the Derwent,
which is there known under the name of the
Grange.   The clouds were hanging heavily on
the surrounding hill-tops, and looked especially
thick in the direction of Scawfell ; but though
our prospects of a good view from the summit
whenever we should get there were hardly re-

assuring, yet having gone so far we were not inclined to beat a retreat, and trusted to "unforeseen contingencies" to explain away the mists which seemed bent on marring our chances of success. It was about twelve o'clock when we started, and we hoped to accomplish the ascent in three hours. We had the choice of two preliminary routes open to us, preliminary because they both led ultimately to the same point, viz., the foot of the Pikes, which we should have to climb from the same side in either case ; the one which was longer and easier, being accessible even to ponies, diverged considerably to the right in the direction of Sty Head Tarn and Sprinkling Tarn ; the other, which was shorter but steeper, led to our left ; we chose the latter. For the first hour our line of march, though very up-hill work, lay entirely over grass-land, varied by bits of marsh, and well irrigated by the numerous little becks which splashed along on all sides of us. The higher we mounted the prettier became the retrospect towards Derwentwater, which looked especially lovely with the green islands dotted here and there over its surface, and its waves having that peculiar flushed appearance which the wind imparts to water when in motion. At half-past one we sat down upon some rocks to eat our luncheon, consisting of hard-boiled eggs and sandwiches, washed down by cold water from a neighbouring rill. Soon after we reached a kind of level plateau, having accomplished the first and easiest half of our journey; from here we caught a glimpse of Windermere, with the sunlight playing on it far away to the east. We had now left grass-land, and the ground we traversed consisted entirely of great blocks of stone piled irregularly one upon another, and having a grey, skeleton-like appearance, in striking contrast with the tufts of lichen that clung to their sides. A spur of Bowfell had first to be surmounted, a pass called Eskhause to be crossed, and at last we were at the foot, not of Scawfell Pike itself, but of the range that collectively bears its name. Foremost of these was Great End, with its long, narrow summit, which we had to climb on one side and descend on the other, only to repeat the process with other and similar ridges which lay in our path. Whilst descending one of these the clouds, which had hitherto persistently shut out all surrounding view, suddenly lifted, and disclosed to our eyes the great pile of Scawfell Pike looming right before us, conspicuous by the hummock of stones erected on its highest point. Here we met some dejected tourists returning from the summit, where they said that they had waited for half-an-hour in hopes that the mist would clear off, but all to no purpose, as they had seen next to nothing; this was rather a gloomy prospect, but we were not to be discouraged, and continued the ascent up a very rocky path, the steepest bit that we had yet climbed, and were at length rewarded by finding ourselves standing on the top of Scawfell Pike. It was half-past three o'clock when we reached the summit. Our first feeling was one of satisfaction at having surmounted all difficulties, and at being for the nonce on a higher elevation than any one else in England; our second, a rapid perception of the fact that it was uncommonly cold. The winds, however calm below, could hardly be expected to retain their serenity at a height of 3208 feet above the level of the sea, and swept round us with a velocity of I-don't-know-how-many miles an hour. So we put on our coats

and wraps, which our guide had been instru-
mental in carrying up for us, and sat down with
our backs to the great cairn, which protected us
from the violence of the wind. Having thus
provided for the outer man, we were able to
look about us. The mountain on which we sat
was a gigantic heap of enormous masses of
loose rock, which one could imagine had either
been thrown up by some pre-historic convulsion
of nature, or swept by a deluge which had
washed away every particle of soil from between
them. The mists curled and wreathed around
us, up through the valleys at our feet to the
mountain tops, which rose in never-ending suc-
cession on all sides of us. Occasionally, as a
sudden gust of wind drove them away, and
during the intervals of sunshine, the view became more extended, and we might well con-
gratulate ourselves on the good fortune that
attended us, for our guide told us that nine
times out of ten one might come up and see
comparatively nothing. Looking towards Borrowdale we could trace the whole line of our
ascent ; beyond Derwentwater the view was
closed by Skiddaw, with not a cloud on its

summit, and second only in importance to
Scawfell itself; a little to its right was Hel-
vellyn, also a king among mountains; still
further to the east lay Windermere, flashing like
a diamond under the rays of the sun in the
dark setting of the surrounding elevations, whilst
far away beyond it we could distinguish the
faint outline of Ingleborough and the Yorkshire
hills. Turning to our left Great Gable frowned
directly before us—a sheer wall of rock from
the path that runs beneath it to its summit
—over which in the distance the Scottish hills
bounded the horizon. A bit of Ireland is sometimes, though very rarely, visible across the
intervening ocean. Our guide had only once
seen it, and the sappers and miners conducting
the Ordnance Survey had been no better
favoured during a stay of nine weeks on the
summit, where we could still see the remains
of the huts which they had erected. On this
occasion the fog brooded heavily over the sea,
and no view was to be obtained in that direction. On the other, or southern side, as the
mists rolled away, Wastwater, which lay almost
immediately below us, was momentarily visible,

with the mountains running straight down to its margin, and, as it were, dipping their feet in its waters, on which a dull grey shimmer rested, hardly to be distinguished from the clouds themselves which enveloped it, and pertinaciously closed again as soon as they had for an instant given way before the driving of the wind. Further to the south we could see Morecambe Bay and the Lancashire coast, the smoke from the chimneys of its manufacturing towns curling straight up in the air, untouched by the winds which raged all around us. The summit of Snowdon has been seen on a very clear day in October, but this was not by any means a clear day, nor was it in the month of October, and our prospect towards the south was very limited.

The nearest mountain to ourselves was Scawfell, not to be confounded with the higher elevation of Scawfell Pike, on which we were standing, and separated from it by Mickledore Chasm, which our guide pointed out to us on the face of the mountain. He had once crossed it, but manifested no inclination to repeat the experiment, although he told us that ladies had

been known successfully to brave its dangers.
After staying for three-quarters of an hour on
the summit we commenced the descent, and had
not proceeded far when our guide bade us look
back at the Isle of Man, pointing the while in
the direction of the sea behind us. He must
veritably have been lynx-eyed, for at first we
could distinguish nothing, and were inclined to
think that he was humbugging us; but on a
sudden the clouds lifted, and there in all truth
lay the island right before us, the range of hills
running down its centre giving it the appearance
of one large mountain, with such an air of sub-
stantiality and propinquity about it that we
could hardly believe that it was some forty-five
miles distant as the crow flies from where we
stood looking at it. A little further down we
caught a glimpse of Crummock Water, one of
the prettiest of the lakes, half hidden away
among the hills. Our line of descent was the
same as that we had followed on our upward
journey till we reached the level plateau which
I have before mentioned, when, instead of going
down Borrowdale, we turned to the right *en*
route for Dungeon Gill. Our day's walk was

not yet over, for, before reaching our goal, we
had to descend a very steep bit called Rosset
Gill. They may say *facilis descensus Averni*,
but this was far from easy, and the Avernus of
the ancients must have been a very different
thing from the Rosset Gill of the moderns.
Jolting of the knee-joints is a most unpleasant
sensation, and we now experienced it to perfection ; we were cheered, however, by the prospect
of a long rest and good cheer as soon as we
reached the bottom, for our hotel was, we were
told, just round the corner.   It is the way of the
world, I suppose, but the " just round the corner "
was more like two miles, and though we each in
turn indignantly repelled the charge, yet we
were thoroughly tired out when, at seven o'clock,
we found ourselves seated in the parlour (coffee-
room is too dignified a name) of the hostelry of
Dungeon Gill.   Food was at once set before us,
and we ate and drank.   I will not go into par-
ticulars.   Suffice it to say that the *menu* was
such as to inspire one of our party with poetical
ideas, and before retiring to bed he had im-
provised and committed to posterity in the
Visitors' Book (a most curious collection of

hieroglyphics), where it may be seen to this day
the following miserable stanza :—

"At Dungeon Gill we had our fill
Of poachèd eggs and bacon ;
The butter'd toast of which they boast
Was certainly no take-in."

I, for my part, couldn't understand the last
line of his effusion, because we "certainly" had
"taken in" considerable amounts of the "poachèd
eggs and bacon ;" so I ended by ascribing it to
the promptings of poetical licence, combined
with the post-prandial effects of the "buttered
toast," and went to bed.

A VALENTINE.

I'M the boat that you have lost,
    Floating down the river,
I'm the boat that you have lost,
    Which you've lost for ever.
I have floated miles away,

Floated, floated many a day,
  Floated down the river,
Past the rapids white with spray,
Past the reaches calm and gray,
I have floated many a day,
  And shall float for ever.

Down the beck I hurried fast,
Down the little beck I pass'd
  Down into the river ;
So I reach'd the sea at last,
  Where I float for ever ;
Storm and rain and tempest-toss'd,
Warp'd by sun and wind and frost,
Floating bottom-uppermost,
I'm the boat that you have lost,
  Which you've lost for ever.

Here for ever shall I float,
Here in waters most remote
  From my own dear river,
Here for ever shall I float,
Most unhappy little boat,
  Float and float for ever ;

If you don't, whate'er the cost,
Answer by return of post,
You'll be haunted by the ghost
Of the boat that you have lost,
Lost perhaps for ever.

SERENADE.

" COME, my pretty capybara,
    Come along with me you must,
Come along with me and share a
    Sixteen-pennyworth of crust.

" Come and see the young opossums
    Sitting in the pleasant shade,
See them crown'd with orange-blossoms,
    Drinking cooling orangeade.

" Come and see the gay gorilla
    Sitting on his mother's knee,
Though so young he soon would kill a
    Maggot or a humble bee.

" See the sweet ornithorhynchus,
　　Who, I hope, is very well ;
Also that he does not think us
　　Far more rude than words can tell.

" Gaze upon the ringtail'd lemur,
　　With what elephantine pride
In a Transatlantic steamer
　　Does it watch the rising tide.

" And observe the armadillo
　　Playing billiards with a cat,
As he leans upon a pillow
　　Slowly putting on his hat.

" Listen to my plaintive metre,
　　Listen to my mournful rhyme,
Shall I tell you how the cheetah
　　Took his morning bath in lime ?

" Shall I tell you how the shepherd
　　Who for long had sought his flock,
Found them all inside a leopard,
　　Basking underneath a rock ?

" But beware, for I shall deem you
 Too extravagant in taste
If you hunt the wily emu,
 Scouring o'er its native waste.

" Do not imitate that quagga,
 Who the zebra's trousers stole,
Merely (so he said) to swagger
 When he call'd upon a mole.

" Firstly, let us make a treaty
 Whensoe'er we see a whale,
For the sake of spermaceti
 Not to pull it by the tail.

" Nor to take it up and skin its
 Head, or hit it on the spine,
Nor to leave it many minutes
 In a glass of boiling wine.

" Come along, and bring your people,
 Come along, I am not proud,
We will sit upon a steeple,
 Gazing on the passing crowd."

Speaking thus the mosasaurus
Vanish'd into empty space,
As a phantom flees before us,
With a smile upon his face.

———

THE MAËLSTROM.

KNOW'ST not thou where in billowy war
The surges beat Lofoden's shore,
But angrier is the sullen roar
    Of the Maëlstrom?

Where bellows in his ocean cell
The Sea-Gnome with a louder yell
Than might resound th' abyss of hell:
    'Tis the Maëlstrom!

Yonder, the rampart of the sky,
A reef-belt thwarts the wilder'd eye,
And echoes back the agony
    Of the Maëlstrom.

Topping the coast, Helseggen's rock
Scornful defies the tempest's shock,
And looks down with an icy mock
        On the Maëlstrom.

The Viking knew its distant hum,
Deep-gotten like a muffled drum,
And cursing said, " I dare not come
        Near the Maëlstrom."

The Norseman sees the frenzied main
Swirling and swelt'ring, writhe in pain,
While rocks give back the wild refrain
        To the Maëlstrom.

The whirlpool seems to knell his doom,
And call him to a watery tomb,
Where opens wide its ghostly womb
        The dread Maëlstrom.

Only a seething frothy heap
Curling around the eddying steep,
As if to girdle in the deep,
        Crowns the Maëlstrom.

Its walls are bright as burnish'd steel,
Its ebon waters circling wheel,
And from the depths with thunder'd peal
                   Cries the Maëlstrom!

Beneath the chaos of its bed
Can mortal tell the myriad dead,
O'er whom the billows harmless tread
                   'Neath the Maëlstrom?

THE FRIAR AND THE FAIRY.

(Appeared in *The Etonian.*)

SIR,—Last holidays, on a tour in a distant
and out-of-the-way country, my friend and I
came upon a secluded valley to which a curious
legend was attached. My friend being of a
poetical turn of mind has shaped the said tale
into what he styles "congenial verse." Moreover he has insisted on its appearing in your
columns; and much against my will I enclose
his rather doubtful production, which he
styles,—

THE FRIAR AND THE FAIRY.

A Legend of St. Holias Damusalensis.

I.

THE FAIRY.

THERE dwelt a Fairy far away,
  Throned on an icy height,
On her ne'er rested golden ray
  Nor fell the folds of night.

Beneath her star-embroider'd veil
  Shone forth her cold blue eyes,
Warm rain around her fell in hail,
  Tears changed to tearless sighs.

All cold and calm the sky above,
  All cold the ice beneath,
All cold and stiff fell eager love
  Beneath her chilly breath.

Nor raging storm nor burning heat
  Disturb'd her calm repose,
Pure blue o'er head, beneath her feet
  The everlasting snows.

In death-like isolation cold
 She ruled the realms of ice,
Far down the sounding valley roll'd
 Her bitter melodies.

" Flow by, O river of life,
 All turbid with maddening hate,
Vain passion, and fury, and strife,
 Vain struggles of lowly and great.

" All bright are thy ripples above,
 But all cold is the current beneath :
Is not hate the destroyer of love ?
 What is life but the victim of death ?

" O river of life, flow by,
 To be lost in the deeps of the sea,
Unscathed of thy fury am I,
 Thy passion is folly to me.

" I have tasted enough of thy sweets,
 I am sick of thy hopes and thy fears,
Vain glory that ever retreats,
 Vain hopes, disappointment, and tears.

" O river of life, flow on,
    Flow on to thy end in the deep ;
Thou too shouldst pass and be gone,
    Leave me here to my passionless sleep."

She sang and smiled a bitter smile,
    With bitter curve of sneering lips,
The aged mountains throbb'd the while,
    And ocean with his myriad ships.

II.

THE FRIAR.

BUT slowly up the valley toil'd,
With threadbare cloak all travel-soil'd,—
That Adam once had worn and Eve'd
Patch'd fifty times, so men believed ;
Yet proof against hell's hottest fire—
A most dilapidated friar.
His step was slow, his back was bent,
For such a practical ascent
Of un-ideal " narrow ways "
Upon the hottest of hot days
He found did not exactly suit
His limbs and years and size to boot.

A man one bitter lesson taught,
Brought up to know one only "ought"
That God above was King of Heaven:
The empire of the world was given
A chosen Man, whose will was law
To bind or loose for evermore.
Who'd calmly doom to endless woe
The struggling race of men below,
Yet labour'd heart and soul to save
Their sinful bodies from the grave.
  Around him flock'd with mocking cries,
And bitter jest and scornful eyes,
The sinful people of the vale,
To hear the pious stranger's tale.

III.

THE METAMORPHOSIS.

FAR off, upon her azure throne,
Who ruled the lonely wastes alone,   -
Her cold brow crown'd with chilly lights,
The icy queen of icy heights,
Heard thunder down the sounding dale,
And proudly pierce the misty veil,

And strike the desert peaks above,
The blessed words of peace and love.
Oh loud and long laugh'd she, "At length,
Pale friar, I measure strength with strength,"
And down the valley terribly
Back whirl'd her mighty melody.

" Echo, re-echo, resounding hills,
    Whisper in answer eternal snow,
Murmuring chant my myriad rills,
    Chant to the craven crowd below.

" Prate poor pedants of peace and love,
    Beauty and virtue, if so ye will,
Prate of predestined heaven above,
    And the freed soul's purity, prate your fill.

" For the rocks will frown and the rivulet flow,
    And the strong rays redden the peaks
        above,
    While man's cold corpse is rotting below,
    With his vain, vain visions of peace and
        love."

She sang, and rock and stream and tree
Caught up the mystic melody,

From rugged peak and tender cloud,
A thousand voices echoed loud,
"While man's pale corpse is rotting below,
   With his vain, vain visions of peace and
     love :"
Broke up the pious congregation,
The Friar's triumphant peroration
On heavenly joys, angelic smiles,
And all the devil's deadly wiles.
Straight ceased the saint, indignant : first
Dares subtle Satan do his worst
With "magic sights and songs accurst :"
And shakes a heaven-abetted fist.
But slowly rose a wreathed mist
And far away he sees uprise
A mighty form, and piercing eyes,
Shedding around a glory cold,
Heart searching, awful to behold.
But bravely o'er her lonely snows
The worthy friar's defiance rose ;
"Thou wilt not live a human life,
Thou hatest human love and strife,
Then there for ever shalt thou sit
All lonely, since thou wishest it :
There throned upon the desert height

For aye enjoy the wish'd delight,
Look down in scorn on men below,
The lonely queen of ice and snow."
He said, and all her awful grace,
Her mystic form and scornful face,
Was slowly stiffen'd,—cold and white
Upon the earth-disdaining height :
Her eyes still gleaming passive hate,
She tower'd in solitary state :
Uncaring she of weal or woe,
A pinnacle of ghastly snow.

A sharp attack of gout next year
Cut short the blessed saint's career.

IHOOD.

(Appeared in *The Etonian.*)

" IHOOD " is a word, readers of *The Etonian*,
learned and unlearned, grave and gay, with
which you are probably as unfamiliar as I was
until the sight of it a day or two ago in an

author of much repute led me to consider it, and so to the conclusion that under other names the matter of its composition is well known to us all. Having acquired which piece of valuable information, after the manner of my egotistical fraternity of scribblers, I could not rest until I had let the world, or at any rate that portion of it which reads *The Etonian*, know of my discovery, heedless whether that discovery were clad in the alluring garb of novelty or not. Perhaps, however, good readers, kind though you be, a guerdon of curses will be mine at your hands if I do not speedily make an end of what you may be pleased to term my conceited circumlocution, and come to the point. The conclusion, then, at which I arrived was that its three component ingredients are each well known under their individual names, but are here fused together in such a form as well illustrates man's subtlety in obscuring the unpleasant realities of life under shadows more or less idealistic.

Firstly. Egoism ; that intense appreciation of self to be observed so frequently both in works and words, both in monkey and man ; that boundless delight that wise men as well as fools take in referring to exploits of their own, usually of the least possible interest to their hearers. People of this nature are apt too to regard any dignity which may be reflected on them by holding a post of trust and honour as proof infallible of their own personal worth, a mistake which occasionally involves them in a quagmire of humiliation. Specimens of the class of egoists, lashed by the powerful pen of Addison, " who delight in repeating as sayings of their own jests which were made before they were born," are occasionally to be met with at Eton and elsewhere.

Secondly. Selfishness, the chillest of all sins. Truly "the wintry cold wherein the mists of selfishness have wrapped the society of men " is a cold which pierces through many a thick garment woven of the good fabric of friendship. Its approach is insidious ; its arrival as fatal to the tender plant of neighbourliness as ever an early frost to the flowers of summer. Not that I would have you suppose, however, that selfishness and heat are incompatible, for somebody says that " extreme self-lovers will set a man's house on fire, though it were but to roast their own eggs." Well, there is plenty of selfishness at Eton in many a garb which it is needless to particularize. *Verbum sapientibus.*

Thirdly. Self-consciousness, which grows a plentiful crop amongst us, in some cases to be pitied, in some ridiculed ; in some cases falling before the sickle of good sense, in others dooming its possessor to perpetual puppydom.

At this point I found myself reflecting that " Ihood " might possibly be also the assertion of Raphael Aben-Ezra's axiom of " I am I ;" an axiom which, if it be not followed by that philosopher's doubts as to whether it should not rather be " I am not I " (for, said he, " am I to be illogical enough to stand up and swear stoutly that I am *one* thing when all I am conscious of is the devil only knows how many things "), ought to lead every one to take especial care that in his own case " I am I " may be an assertion of which he shall have no call to be ashamed ; a thing easily done if the " I " divested of its " hood " will connect itself with the Thou, " our relations to whom in their manifold varieties are the source of all our affections and all our duties."

LINES AT THE RIVER SIDE,

SHOWING HOW THE POET WAS UNFORTU-
NATELY DISAPPOINTED OF A MOST TRAGIC
THEME.

'TIS but a work of the loom,
  'Tis but a shawl on the grass,
  'Tis but a remnant, alas !
Remnant of what and of whom ?

Surely some victim of woe
  Left it to bleach on the brink,
  Left it to plunge and to sink
Under the waters below.

Doubt, hesitation, and fear,
  Madness, delusion, despair,
  All of them culminate there,
There by the swift-rushing weir.

Was it a husband she fled,
  Drunken, of reason bereft ?
  Was it a child that she left
· Peaceful and pale in its bed ?

Rash was the folly, I trow,
   Vice got the best of the strife.
   One little moment of life !
What would she give for it now ?

Ha ! what has shatter'd it all ?
   How is my Muse disarray'd ?
   Only a nursery-maid
Come back to look for her shawl.

———————

ARIADNE.

So all day long she roam'd about the beach
And listen'd to the moaning of the sea
Splashing upon the rocks ; above, the sky
Was blue, as is the violet in the spring ;
Behind her lay the isle all beautiful
Like unto Paradise ; for then it was
The morning of the world, and everything
Was young. But she alone was desolate ;
The murmuring zephyrs fann'd her beauteous
   face,

The gentle waves fell cooling her small feet,
The vines entwined her with their soft embrace,
Trying to stay her ; aloft the fair sun shone,
The sea-birds wheel'd around with circling flight,
Like happy souls departed of the blest,
But she mourn'd on, there was no happiness
For her in happy nature, but she still
Heard only the soft moaning of the sea
And wander'd desolate along the beach.

"ANGLE TARN."

A REMINISCENCE OF THE CUMBERLAND LAKE
DISTRICT.

HIGH above the distant ocean,
   Deep embosom'd in the hills,
Sleeps a tarn, unknown to legend,
   Fed by countless tiny rills.

Mountain-girt its cold blue waters
   Seem to tell a dreamy tale
Of some by-gone generation
   When the eve begins to pale.

And, as twilight's shadows deepen
  O'er the surface of the mere,
In its wavelets frown reflected
  Beetling heights of mountain sere.

But when night reigns undisputed,
  Silver'd by the rising moon,
Like an evening star it glitters,
  Or the Sun-God at his noon.

Rather would I see it crested
  Billow-like with flakes of foam,
When the thunder's boom re-echoes
  Through the fortress of its home ;

When its murky waves are smitten
  By the flash of Heaven's fire,
And the darkling hills illumined,
  Like the blaze of funeral pyre.

Oft the shepherd stays to wonder
  At the grandeur of the scene,
Either side the cloud-capp'd summits,
  And the storm-toss'd lake between.

Homeward then he faster presses
    To his cabin on the fell,
And his rugged heart is soften'd
    As it were by magic spell.

But when Morning's voice awakens,
    Hush'd is then the tempest'sroar,
And the whirlwind, baffled, crouches
    In its cavern on the tor.

Dark as this is life of mortals
    When the clouds o'erset its sky,
Brighter far as gleam its billows,
    Prescient of eternity.

MEA CULPA;

OR,

THE WRONG NOTE IN THE WRONG ENVELOPE.

My fault, it burns my soul within,
    But I would die unshriven ;
Though thus to those who greatly sin
    Are all their sins forgiven.

Lo! I may bidden be to live
  Eternally in pain ;
But 'tis less blessed so to give
  Than such a gift to gain.

For, so I have more time to hate,
  My pain will be forgot ;
Though madd'ning torments round me wait,
  Though fires of hell be hot.

I loved him with a perfect love,
  Kept secret for his sake ;
But oft where seems to brood a dove
  Lies coil'd a poisonous snake.

'Twas in the garden when the dusk
  Was blotting out the trees,
And heavy with the fragrant musk
  Whisper'd the evening breeze,

A rose-bud wreath fell at my feet,
  Nestled a note within ;
And in my cheeks the sudden heat
  Confess'd the secret sin.

But shuddering horror shook my heart,
    I sank upon my knee,
Discovering, with a sudden start,
    The note was not for me.

It seem'd as if upon my ear
    There peal'd a tolling bell ;
For not for me the letters clear,
    The hand I knew so well.

As if the fiend, while yet the knell
    Disturb'd the silent air,
Had reach'd a horrid hand from hell,
    And caught me by the hair.

I sought the wood upon the height,
    The place his note assign'd ;
I climb'd the cliff with aspect light,
    And murder in my mind.

I stood upon the steepest hill,
    Above a wall of rock,
And watch'd the blackening rookery fill
    With its funereal flock.

I waited veil'd beneath the shade
  Till the deceiver came,
And his false arms about me laid,
  And lisp'd another's name;

And gently lifted up my veil
  Another's cheek to kiss;
I saw his eyes beneath me quail,—
  I hurl'd him down th' abyss.

Still on my ears the echo rings,
  The shriek of deadly fright;
The startled rooks on heavy wings
  Flapp'd off into the night.

And, priest, now I've avenged my wrong
  In that victorious strife,
What boots the minutes to prolong?
  What reck I of my life?

HARD TO BEAR.

The day was bright, the day was fair,
When pass'd a little polar bear
  From out his home of ice;

He look'd around with air profound,
Survey'd the nature of the ground,
  And thought it very nice.

His hair was white, his claws were long ;
'Twas not (in his opinion) wrong
  To leave his mother old,
And wander off and play the fool
With everything so nice and cool—
The climate there is (as a rule)
  Frigid, as I've been told.

He said, " I'll hunt the finny seal
  And drive him from his lair,
And thence prepare a mid-day meal
  For this here little bear."
He call'd himself " this little b."
He *might* have said, " for little me ;"
But yet it is a fact that he
  Said, " for this little bear."

Perhaps you think our hero found
  The amusement that he sought ;
Then reader, empty hopes you ground
  On what you didn't ought.

His bones lie hid beneath a mound ;
He is a thing of nought ;
His mother in a glacial cave
Weeps for the son she could not save.

———

AN ETON LOWER-BOY ;

*Being another and shorter version of " A Day of
my Life."*

IN 5 SCENES.

Scene 1. The Eton boy peacefully slumbers in
his bed ; the bed is situated in a small apartment, which he calls by the distinctive title of
" his " room ; the room in question is one on
the right or maybe the left side of a long passage, whose walls are pierced at equal distances
by the doorways of similar retreats, in which
sleep other Eton Boys like himself. The passage forms an entire story in a house, the
chief external features of which are archi-
tectural ugliness, abnormal height, and bricks of
a brilliant cochineal hue. To return to the Eton

Boy. It is 7 a.m. An unwelcome apparition, familiarly known as a boy's-maid, flashes into the room, rattles up the rather flimsy and feebly-squeaking green blind, awakens the still sleeping youth with a shout, and decamps with the same precipitancy and total disregard of surroundings as she just now entered. The occupant of the bed heaves a slumber-teeming sigh, slowly opens his eyes, thinks he will just take another snooze before getting up, turns round for that purpose, and relapses into the outstretched arms of Morpheus . . . . Suddenly with a convulsive start he wakes, roused by the trampling of feet upon the wooden staircase outside, and the general commotion attendant on the turning out of some forty boys first thing in the morning. Confusedly he dashes out of bed, hastily he washes, still more hastily he robes, furiously he jams his chimney-pot hat on his head, wildly he snatches up some books, and he is gone! The room lacks its presiding genius; silence prevails.

Scene 2. Some thirty youths, seated on benches, their books open at the wrong place on the desk before them, are marshalled under the eye of a tall stern-looking man in a black gown, whose tones, whether of correction, rebuke, or command, ring out with an unpleasant clang in the keen morning air. The door opens very gently, a small and particularly untidy-looking boy slinks in very cautiously, and with wonderful celerity of movement and subtlety of action drops into his vacant seat.

Master. *I* see you. Write out 200 lines of the 2nd Æneid, and bring them—

Boy. Please, Sir, I—

Master. Don't " Please, Sir " me ! and bring them to my house—

Boy. Please, Sir, I wasn't called.

Master. To my house before two o'clock.

Boy. Please, Sir !

Master. Do it twice !

(Suppressed whistle round the room).

Scene 3. Another, and rather superior-looking apartment in the house that has before been introduced to the reader. A tall youth, the consciousness of immense importance and consequent *nonchalance* manifest in his every feature as well as action, stands with his coat-tails elevated, warming his back before the fire, and

superintending the somewhat confused movements of three or four little boys, all vieing with
each other in obsequiousness to the "great and
complete man," and in the execution of his
commands. This constitutes the process called
" mess-fagging." Small boy A. · spreads the
cloth. Small-boy B. (whom we already know),
endeavours to arrange symmetrically the crock-
ery upon it, and in doing so contrives to smash
a cup and saucer (for which he receives imme-
diate punishment at the hands of the individual
before the fire). Small-boy C. is despatched to
do some toast and boil some eggs ; after an interval he returns, the toast like a brick, the eggs
as to their internals not unlike liquid gum. The
fagmaster, who has meanwhile been endeavouring
to promote by sedulous manipulation the growth
of a few capillary bristles just starting into existence on that part of his cheek immediately below
the lobe of the ear, being acquainted with the
modest culinary capabilities of the fag, says not
a word, but merely helps him to leave the room
with a sympathetic movement of his leg. Exeunt
A. B. C. Tall youth is left alone to foster the
afore-mentioned appendages in solitude.

Scene 4.—B. (whose movements on the day in question we follow) descends to the small room in which he first appeared. The bed before prostrate, has now by a process peculiar to itself been crumpled up, framework and all, into its shell, and as an article of furniture forms one of the most commanding ornaments of the room. A few remarks on the latter may not be out of place. Its chief contents in addition to the bed are a *bureau* with pigeon-holes and desk above, some books carelessly chucked on the latter standing out like a lacustrine village in the sea of ink peacefully floating around them, and taking its source from a bottle which has been knocked over in the prevalent chaos ; drawers below, containing the wardrobe of the owner, whose name is sliced in huge and somewhat unshapely Capitals on the outer surface. This piece of furniture goes by the name of the *burry*. Opposite to it on the other side of the room is a bookcase of corresponding build, and known as the *book-burry*. On the top of both are sundry little china and earthenware pots, bought as old Worcester at enormous prices from enterprising shop-dealers of the neighbourhood, and all in a more or less dilapidated condition ; the other moveables are a table in the window, of which more presently, a couple of chairs of a rather primitive type, and a small washstand in the corner. On the walls hang some gorgeous prints and brilliantly painted photographs, mostly representations of scenes in the chase ; the grass in the foreground preternaturally green, the fox with a huge brush walking about in the distance, the hounds almost on each other's backs, endeavouring to scale a wall of formidable altitude, over which one horseman is sailing in mid air, while another flounders in the lubricating toils of a cesspool the other side, and yet another, his lately abandoned steed watching his movements with interest over the top of the wall, is describing an aerial parabola, which, judging from the direction of his head, must infallibly result in the considerable discomfort, if not the utter destruction, of the latter. Such are the *tableaux vivants* that illuminate the principal wall of this Etonian's retreat ; elsewhere we notice the familiar " Challenge," with its comrade the equally familiar " Sanctuary," both a little distorted by the unsparing brush of the artist, whose improvements

I

on the original picture have been executed with
a view to brilliant atmospheric effect, and striking antithesis of colour.   An Eton Almanack, a
photograph-caricature of his tutor nailed on to
the wall in the place of honour, and a few other
minor illustrations, and the tale of the walls is
done.

To revert to the table before alluded to.   On it
is a breakfast cloth originally white, now blotched
with innumerable parti-coloured stains ; the fare
consists of a couple of pheasants, a rabbit-pie, and
a ham, all brought from home, a rolled Paysandu
ox-tongue (whatever that may be) and some
truffled larks (supposed synonym for potted
blackbirds) procured from the grocer in the town.
Met to enjoy this repast are small boy B. and
his mess-mate, answering in many respects to
the private school "chum."   For ten minutes they
eat hard : a dispute arises : words first of contempt, second of derision, third of insult, fourth
of actual provocation are bandied from side to
side : bread and sugar fly through the air.   "You
scug," says A.   "Tu quoque," says B.   Personal
violence is resorted to ; A. is ejected ; B., in the
exultation of victory, smooths his hair, puts on his

hat, which has been furiously kicked about in the recent struggle, and goes to chapel.

Scene 5. Chapel over, B. returns with pacific intention towards A. They meet ; A., humiliated by the lately inflicted defeat, is anxious for reconciliation ; B. is not averse ; a simple equation is concluded, and the affair clenched by A. offering to "sock" B. With this object in view, like the original "Arcades ambo" they stroll "down town" into the far-famed Webber's. (The next stage of their proceedings is a little harrowing to people of delicately strung nerves, and had better be left unperused by matrons who have at heart the abdominal welfare of their sons.)

A. " What will you have ? "

B. " Let's see " (looks at *Menu*), " Welsh rabbit, oyster and chicken and ham patties, lobster croquets, tarts and cream, ginger and cream, strawberry cream and lemon water! May as well begin at the beginning and go straight through ? "

A. " All right ! "

    *   *   *   *   *

After the lapse of about half an hour they

emerge, A., who has stood the treat, *minus* about five shillings, both of them with a feeling of oppression about the stomach, eminently suggestive in their opinion of the *summum bonum* of bodily enjoyment.

The further movements of A. and B. on this day the writer has no time and the reader probably no inclination to follow. Possibly the afternoon was but a repetition of the morning, the feats of the latter but a foretaste of greater achievements in the former. It is debilitating in the extreme to read of the youthful Etonian beginning the day with 200 lines of the second Æneid, and requiring the assistance of Webber to help him through the earlier part of it. What, then, would not be the state of prostration entailed by the information that another 200 lines and further bodily support marked the waning hours of the afternoon? Perhaps it may have been so, and perhaps it may not. Anyhow, at half-past ten in the evening the troubles and joys of the day are merged in the dreams of night. The young Etonian slumbers. If you will let me, so will I.

———

EARLY SCHOOL.

IF there is a vile, pernicious,
    Wicked, and degraded rule,
Tending to debase the vicious,
    And corrupt the harmless fool :
If there is a hateful habit
    Making man a senseless tool,
With the feelings of a rabbit,
    And the wisdom of a mule:
It's the rule which inculcates
It's the habit which dictates
The wrong and sinful practice of going into school.

If there's anything improving
    To an erring sinner's state,
Which is useful in removing
    All the ills of human fate :
If there's any glorious custom
    Which our faults can dissipate,
And can casually thrust 'em
    Out of sight, and make us great :
It's the plan by which we shirk
Half our matutinal work,
The glorious institution of always being late.

"IT WAS A DREAM."

TOWARDS the close of a weary day, I wearily sat in the weariest of places, viz. one of the mathematical school-rooms. And here let me remark that it is most devoutly to be hoped that the new rooms will be better—worse they cannot possibly be. I tried to write poetry, but failed to produce anything but the following miserable couplet :—

> " I toil'd, I rack'd my weary brain,
> With studying the Inclined Plane."

I said the couplet was miserable ; miserable is not the word for it ; but it admirably expressed the state of my feelings, and its wretchedness harmonized well with mine, and that of the surrounding scenery.

So I tried to write prose : but it was worse, if possible, than what I am writing now. So I added to my catalogue of offences one worse than all the rest, and crowned my iniquity by GOING TO SLEEP. As if to punish me, my dream was intensely, disgustingly mathematical. I dreamt that I was $\pm \sqrt{-1}$ and that I was sitting alone on an Inclined Plane made of ice, and surrounded by a group of admiring, but impatient mathematicians. Then for the first time I realized the feelings of the water which Tantalus could not drink, and though that feeling was not so *very* bad after all, I was harassed by a miserable uncertainty as to whether I was positive or negative. Besides, one gentleman, who had nearly squared the circle at least 100 times, questioned my existence altogether, which was annoying to say the least of it. Another one (I fancy his name was Du Moivre, and that he had a theorem, which is a habit of some people) remarked, " Never mind, we do not want to know its value, we can get on without that : it is merely an imaginary quantity." " Sir," said I, " I object to being called ' *it.*' " This made him collapse, and he became a logarithm. *He* always was very positive. Then all the others ran away to see a fight between a parallelopiped and a quadratic equation. The equation won, and I discovered to my horror they had been fighting about me. So now I belonged to the equation, and was its answer. Perhaps you have never been an answer, in which case you cannot be expected to know what it feels like. However,

the filthy quadratic could not get at me, because
it could not solve the ice. So I. Todhunter, Esq.,
came and squared me by trigonometry with a
theodolite, and so I became — 1, i. e. I was so
much not there, that even if I had been, I should
have been somewhere else. The place I had
got to varied inversely as quick as it could, pro-
ducing a feeling of nausea, which was not relieved
by hearing a voice tell me that I was asleep, nor
much alleviated by the horrid result, which was
that I awoke.

A "FUGITIVE" PIECE.

February, 1876.

THE negro from bondage escaped,
  And flying the slave-holder's law,
Has ever been look'd on as safe
  In one of our own men-of-war.

He was safe from the hunters of men,
  The bloodhound, the yoke, and the whip;
He once more was a freeman again
  On the deck of a true British ship.

But manners and times have all changed,
  And our policy's suffer'd a check,
And lately Ward Hunt has arranged
  He no longer shall stand on that deck.

You will start—and I freely allow
  That nothing at first can seem stranger ;
But remember, an ironclad now
  Is a place of most serious danger.

They "ram " one another so fast,
  In a moment before you are thinking,
That there scarcely is time at the mast
  To run up the signal "We're sinking."

The water runs in at their ports,
  And they sink to the bottom like lead ;
In vain all ingenious resorts
  To raise them once more from their bed.

So it's better the slave should remain
  With his owner and master fast bound,
For if once on our ships it is plain
  You may lay the long odds that he's drown'd.

FROM PINDAR, OLYMP. II.

Ay, gold's pure gold in the hand of the just,
　Gold in the hand of the good is power ;
　An eager mood and a deep her dower,
A star far seen, a beacon of glory,
　A light wherein is a hero's trust.
　If but he knoweth what shall be
　Under the earth, beyond the tomb,
　The doom of the dead, the certain doom,
Knoweth the judgment old in story
　Of all that the eye of Zeus can see :
　There he judges by hard constraint,
　Weary of crime and earthly taint ;
There he judges, the old judge hoary,
　There he judges, and who can flee ?

But the good shall forget their travail and toil
　For ever inwrapt in calm sunlight,
　In day's sweet breath and glory of night,
Where never awakes the dull sea moaning,
　Nor hard hands violent vex the soil :
　The tearless meed of the blameless past,

Of steadfast faith is the hero's now,
And the high gods circle the weary brow,
The weary limbs by their side enthroning
In the sweet new world that is his at last.
But the blasted eye must turn away
And the shivering heart recoil, men say,
From the dread abyss where the lost lie groaning
In writhing passion eternal cast.

Then whosoever have dared to stand
Thrice stand firm both sides of the grave,
Thrice from all sin his soul to save,
Shall tread Jove's path to his father's towers,
The towers of Cronos, the blooming land ;
Wherever the ocean breezes blow,
Blow and whisper and sink to rest,
And down by the sweet burnside the Blest
Weave their circlet of clustering flowers,
Or scatter the tall bough's golden glow ;
For such is the Judge's just command,
Whom Cronos holds at his own right hand,
Cronos, the lord of thrones and powers,
And Rhea, queen of the world below.

———

ELEÄNORE.

BEYOND the Western Main
Her lily life did wane,
> Eleänore.

Her soul pass'd through the night
Towards the morn of light,
> Eleänore.

They tomb'd her in the deep,
To sleep no mortal sleep,
> Eleänore.

The billows seem to wail,
Ah ! could their voice avail
> Eleänore !

The Mistral's icy breath
Shriek'd out the song of death,
> Eleänore.

Mingled amid the surge,
Wind, waves, repeat the dirge—
> Eleänore.

Below, the coral-bed
Pillows about her head,
   Eleänore.

On earth, alone am I,
Oh! for the by-and-by,
   Eleänore !

LINES WRITTEN AT "PRIVATE."

IT is very dull no doubt
 Hearing Wh—ll—y prate,
Dull to hear K—n—ly spout
 When he grows irate,
Dull to be harangued about
 Nuns by N—wd—g—te.
Very dull is all of this,
 Very dull and dry,
But it is surpass'd, I wis,
 Most completely by
" Caii Julii Cæsaris
 Commentarii."

OUR COLLEGE BREWERY.

Burnt down in November, 1875.

(Appeared in *The Etonian.*)

OUR College Brewery is no more, but the following lines—an extract from one of our most celebrated poets—may serve to remind our readers that the public was licensed to be drunk on its premises, when it sold, as well as brewed, the College beer.

THE LICENSED VITTLER.

Goldsmith's " Deserted Drunkard."

Near yonder yard, where once the brewery
    smiled,
And still where many a brewer's tub lies piled ;
There, where a few black boards the place
    disclose,
The Little Vittler's modest mansion rose.
A man he was to all the College dear,
And sating all with quarts of poison'd beer,
Remote from " Reid's " he ran his godly race,
Nor e'er had changed, nor wish'd to change his
    place ;

Unskilful he to fawn, or seek for power,
Like pastors fashion'd to the varying hour;
Far other aims his heart had learnt to praise,
More bent to sate the drunken than to raise.
His house was known to all the vagrant worst,
He chid their wanderings, but relieved their
    thirst;
The long-remember'd drunkard was his guest,
Who, paying little, took on tick the rest.
The ruin'd spendthrift, now no longer drunk,
Claim'd kindred there, with cheeks and eyelids
    shrunk;
The broken soldier, kindly bade to stay,
Sat by his fire, and drank the night away;
Wept o'er his thirst, or, thirst and dryness done,
Shoulder'd his crutch, and round in frenzy spun:
Pleased with his guests the good man learn'd to
    grin,
And quite forgot their vices in their gin.
Careless their merits or their faults to scan,
His money got ere drinking-time began.
Thus to relieve the thirsty was his pride,
And e'en his failings lean'd to pity's side;
But in his duty prompt at every call,
He watch'd and peep'd, enticed and flatter'd all.

And, as a fox each fond endearment tries,
To tempt a crow-borne dainty from the skies,
He tried each heart, reproved each dull delay,
Allured to gas-lit rooms, and led the way.
There, on the floor, where parting life was laid,
And sorrow, thirst, and pain, by turns dismay'd,
The Little Vittler stood.   At his command
Both cash and life fast fled the struggling
      hand;
"Allsopp" flow'd down the trembling wretch to
      floor,
And his last faltering accents whisper'd "More!"
At home, with meek and unaffected grin,
His looks adorn'd his venerable chin;
Scorn from his lips prevail'd with double blink,
And fools, who came to cant, remain'd to
      drink.
The service past, around the little man,
With ready zeal, each thirsty Christian ran;
E'en small boys follow'd his provoking sneer,
And robb'd their purse, to share the good man's
      beer.
His ceaseless grin a flatt'rer's warmth express'd,
Their thirst well pleased him, and their fears
      distress'd;

To them, his Bass, his Reid, his X were given,
But all his serious thoughts sought golden
leaven.
As some small pug, that lifts its awful form,
Swells with proud breast, and squeaks above the
storm,
Though round his path the College flung their
curse,
Perpetual pennies dropp'd into his purse.

SOCK-CADS.

ANY one at all acquainted with Eton can
hardly have failed to observe that certain parts
of College are at times infested by a class of
men, who are at once a great discredit to the
school, an eyesore to the authorities, and a
snare to the " students." It will be seen that we
allude to the " Sock-cads," those vendors of the
enticing strawberry, the captivating chocolate,

K

and the alluring bun. It would be but waste of
time to descant on the manners and customs of
these tradesmen, for we can hardly imagine
that the amount of the former, and the nature of
the latter, is unknown to any of our readers.
But we know too well that but few realize the
pernicious effects that such a traffic is likely to
bring about. Perhaps they will think this subject beneath their notice ; we do no think that
it is—there is no reason why we should pass over
all that relates to seemingly trivial occurrences.
Let it be clearly understood that we do not
mean to imply that there is naturally anything
very vicious or degrading in the casual enjoyment of desultory refreshment. Far from it ;
and even though small boys do occasionally
make themselves ill by an over-indulgence of
appetite, it would be in the highest degree unjust
to lay to the charge of the vendor what so
obviously arises from the folly of the purchaser.
If this class of tradesmen did not exist at Eton,
this evil would, of course, be to a great extent
obviated ; but if any one supposes that one of
these men will say, " You have had as much as
is good for you, I cannot sell you any more," he

expects a disinterested generosity and a noble sacrifice of self not found except in the most exalted of spirits.

Easily, then, we can, and do, acquit the Sock-cads of this charge; but this is not all. We cry out, and we hope that every public-spirited Etonian will cry out against the iniquitous system of "ticking." To the conscientious tradesman this system does not bring profit; for it is obvious that, if he does not charge more than is fair, he cannot make much money, unless all his customers are as honourable as himself. As a matter of fact, the honour of the customers, though it may not come up to the standard of the ideal tradesman, far surpasses that of the sordid and degraded Sock-cad "as he is." It would be bad, indeed, for Eton, if it did not. No one can be ignorant that the loss arising from non-payment is more than amply made up for by the exorbitant tariff of charges, and by the interest that unaccountably accumulates on unpaid bills during the short interval of the holidays. A boy eats, perhaps, five shillings' worth in the course of a school-time; next half there awaits him a bill for 13*s.* 7½*d.*, always the

$\frac{1}{2}d.$ to make a show of scrupulous accuracy and consummate exactness.

Perhaps he does not much mind paying this when he is flush of cash; but is this an argument in favour of such extortion being permitted to exist? Ought not the Sock-cads to be obliterated? If they were ornamental and did no harm, their existence might on the whole be desirable; but now they are not only neither useful nor ornamental, but they are absolutely pernicious. We do not know, of course, who are responsible, or whether any one is responsible, for the abolition of nuisances of this kind; but we would suggest that some steps should be taken to prevent our College being disfigured by the presence of unsightly objects such as those we have been discussing.

A CHARACTER.

" Before the beginning of years
There came to the making of man."

THE World, the Flesh, the Devil once
Agreed to patronize a dunce,
And make his sorry dulness shine
With splendid sparkle half divine.
" My gift is trousers," lisp'd the World,
As curlier yet his tail he curl'd ;
And neatly posing, half aloof,
Scann'd at his ease a blameless hoof.
" I give the mystic charm of dress,
True sesame of nobleness ;
And if so much is given to me,
Your most Satanic majesty,
I give him trousers, and a tongue
To charm the vilest wretch unhung,
Rehearsing with unwonted praise
His little *specialités.*
To win as soon the would-be wise
Prating of ' earthly vanities,'
Of virtue, ' joy of men and gods '
In earth-disdaining periods,

Against some pet abuse to rage
In fulminating verbiage,
With solemn saws and rapid rant,
Alike on heaven and hell descant,
With enviable sway to rule
Each pedant prig or fulsome fool.
But p'raps I trespass here again
On my Satanic friend's domain."
Here ceased the courteous World, and then
The Flesh and Satan said "Amen."
Thereon the Flesh proceeded : "This
Shall constitute his perfect bliss,
To lose all life and power and sense
In undisturbèd indolence.
Him shall no hot ambition fire,
No angry spur of sharp desire
Shall goad his slow reluctant soul
To race towards the distant goal.
The stroke of seven his only care,
His paradise an easy chair ;
This gift, my friends, seems best to me,
Unbounded *vis inertiæ.*"
Here smiled the World politest praise,
And wish'd he too, in former days,

Had had, to form *his* character,
So wise a ghostly godfather ;
But would his majesty proceed ?
His gift would be a gift indeed.
Thereon proceeded Satan : " I
Could hardly hope to soar so high,
Or such abysmal deeps descend
As can my soul-discerning friend ;
But still I give, as lord of lies,
That golden gift which all men prize,
That all desire so mightily,
The golden gift of Courtesy.
The power to analyze the heart,
Discern and weigh each feebler part.
For him the most reserved shall prate,
For him the foibles of the great,
Each grosser thought and mean delight,
Each silly love and petty spite,
Whatever's vile and mean and low,
Shall in his presence stronger grow.
Sin's faithful friend and virtue's foil
Round every heart 'tis his to coil ;
With smoothest tongue and ready ear
To check or guide each hope and fear,

Alike the bad and good to turn
To his own purposes, and learn
The secrets of the human heart,
To better play his petty part.
This gift, this power, seems best to me ;
This heaven-corrupting courtesy,
Which earth and hell alike can bless,
The golden gift of oiliness."
And so these faithful friends agreed
In wisest ways a soul to lead ;
The charms of Flesh, the potent pride
Of World for him is exercised,
The Devil's most æsthetic cult,
And —— was the blest result.

"SWAGGERS."

FOR a novice in Eton life it would not be an easy matter to explain accurately and discriminately what is meant by the word "swagger," as applied to the swell portion of the Eton community, nor to define its latitude. I propose to do so, adopting as my plan of action a division into three sections. I would, however, make a few preliminary remarks on the limitation of the word. It is one which can by no means be universally applied : on the contrary, it is the prerogative of a few, and those not necessarily in the same part of the school. A new boy regards with intuitive respect all such exalted personages, makes it his first point to become acquainted with their names, looks upon it as rather an honour to be " fagged " by them, speaks of them with admiring awe. None but their most intimate friends presume to speak to them unless addressed in the first place. A place in " Pop " is eagerly sought for, as being a sure admittance to such a life ; still more so a cane. Excellence in games is likely to procure this celebrity. But I am encroaching on my first section, to which I now proceed :—

I.—This consists of those who have fairly earned the sobriquet by their acknowledged superiority at cricket, boating, or football, as many as have their Eleven, Eight, or Field Colours, and, maybe, can appear in a different cap every day of the week. These walk about arm-in-arm, with slow and stately tread ; if overcome by heat, they may with impunity tilt the hat over the back of the forehead ; they are neat in dress, not gaudy : many of them assume " stick-ups," as soon as they have reached this the last stage of their ambition at Eton. They are nearly all of them members of " Pop," before which distinguished assembly they display their sparkling eloquence in impromptu orations once a week. They assiduously cultivate whiskers, if they can find the slightest sign of such capillary appendages on the cheeks. In fine, they are the Presiding Spirit of Eton Society, which could not flourish without them.

II.—In this section are enrolled all literary " swells," fellows who have attained a high place in the school, either by their natural talents or by hard work ; and whose ambition it is to climb the topmost pinnacle of Sixth Form honour. In this position they are regarded with as much admiration by small boys in general as that attached to " Swaggers " of the first order. Those keep up the athletic, these the literary repute of the school, as well here as at the Universities, to which the majority of them proceed on leaving Eton. The ranks of this class are

always well filled, volunteers never failing to step
into the gaps caused by the departure of their
predecessors; a contrast to those of No. 1
Section, whose numbers fluctuate considerably,
there being always more aspirants to its mem-
bership in the summer half than at any other
time of the year. A character which combines
the essential components of both these classes,
is a rare occurrence, an adept at out-door pursuits
finding it hard to pay much attention to his
studies.

III.—I ought not, perhaps, to have included
the members of this division in my category of
" swaggers." I might, indeed, with a greater
show of truth, call them "pseudo-swaggers," for
such is their proper appellation. I allude to the
" patent-leather-booted swell," if I can prefix such
an epithet to his name. He is more exalted in
his own estimation than in that of other people;
no doubt he thinks himself infallible, an opinion
in which he has, fortunately, very few consentients.
Self-appearance is his chief study. Examining
him from head to foot, I find that as a rule he
wears a hat with a highly elevated brim, an admirably folded tie; his coat tightly buttoned across

his chest with some four buttons, cuffs projecting a good two inches beyond his coat-sleeve, pantaloons of gorgeous hue and surprising texture. This is perhaps rather an exaggerated specimen of his race ; smaller editions of the same are, however, frequent. They are of neither intellectual nor athletic tastes : they may have a smattering of either, which, however, they do not care to develope.

There is yet another class, which, however, I have purposely omitted, as having no limitation : it comprises fellows who are on their way to the first section, but are as yet in the chrysalis state, whence they will eventually emerge into the full-grown butterfly. Its numbers are larger than any of the three other classes, its members more widely separated.

FROM OXFORD TO ETON IN CANOES.

A Trip made by three Eton boys in the Summer of 1875.

ABOUT eleven o'clock on one of the lovely mornings in the early part of August, which formed such a delightful contrast to the many rainy days which this year immediately succeeded St. Swithin, a party of three might have been seen standing on one of the Oxford barges, equipped in various extraordinary costumes, such as are usually to be met with on our large rivers at this season of the year. These three individuals (a staid and respected schoolfellow of mine, whom on the *lucus a non lucendo* principle I shall call Easy, my minor, and myself) were at length about to carry out a long-entertained project of going from Oxford to Windsor *à la Canoe*, having previously spent a very pleasant week in the Volunteer Camp at Claydon. Easy being the eldest of the party, and of a somewhat crotchety steadiness, was installed as "leader," a position which he proved himself well fitted to occupy ; for being a well-developed "wetbob" and afflicted with slight temporary insanity (which is indeed said by envious "dry-bobs" to be a characteristic of the "wetbob" community generally), it was some time before he could be brought to see that, according to our ideas, an enjoyable trip did not consist in continually trying to ascertain the racing capacities of the respective canoes.

None of us had ever been more than a hundred yards in a canoe before, and our somewhat unsteady gait and erratic course at starting furnished material for sundry gibes and jeers to certain evil-disposed urchins on the bank. We got through our first two locks, Iffley and Sandford, in good time, but between the latter place and that most lovely spot Nuncham, whose beauties must be seen to be realized, our pace was but little faster than that of the current

One o'clock came, but with it, alas! came no signs of Abingdon, where we had determined to lunch, and it was not until 2.30 that we found ourselves on *terra firma*, and actually seven miles on our water road.

"I don't know what you fellows were about this morning," said Easy in an injured tone, as

we sat down to lunch, "but if you don't make up
your minds to go rather faster than two miles an
hour, we shan't get to Wallingford to-night, nor
to Eton by Friday." " Well," said we, "we didn't
suppose we should, but we would try, and if we
didn't succeed, we could not help it." However,
we hurried over our lunch, and then went to see
the quaint old almshouses, near the river, which
well repaid a visit, enlivened as they were by the
"chatteration" of a friendly old dame, who told
us a little that was worth knowing and a great
deal that was not, about her charge.

Four o'clock found us a quarter of a mile
below Abingdon ; but after passing Culham
Lock the temptation of allowing the stream to
take us down without any exertion on our part
proved too much for two of us, and we accordingly floated over the somewhat long reach that
intervenes between Culham and Clifton, amusing
ourselves meanwhile with singing, to the ap-
parent astonishment and disgust of sundry rustic
piscators. We had tea at the " Barley Mow
Inn," at Clifton—a quaint little hostelry, near
a most beautiful part of the river ; but our staid
leader—deaf to our pathetic entreaties and

protestations that we should never get to Wallingford without his protecting care—started off
by himself, before he had swallowed more than
a mouthful, muttering something unintelligible
about the evening vapours of a river, as if we
were in an African swamp, and followed by the
somewhat uncharitable observation that "two
are company, but three are none."

My minor and I left Clifton about seven, and
were unlucky enough to get into the next locks
with an unwieldly Leviathan, in the shape of a tim-
ber barge, which delayed us considerably. The
mouth of the Thame, which we passed about a
mile below Day's Lock, was very like the entrance
to Cuckoo Weir stream, at "Bargemans;" but
we had not time to explore it.

Dorchester, with its old abbey church and
Roman remains, we saw among the trees, but
dearly as we should have liked to prove ourselves akin to that proverbial and much ma-
ligned personage, the British tourist, we had to
deny ourselves the pleasure of a visit to what
was once one of the chief Roman towns in
Britain.

On, on we went, passing the lovely four miles

of river between Day's Lock and Bensington
in the calm stillness of an August evening ; on
past the eyots that abound in this part of the
river, under Shillingford Bridge, past many
" brethren of the angle," in punts, learning
patience, and perhaps at the same time

> ' To read the words of love
> That shine o'er Nature's page,"

on past Rush Court and the Ferry—until just as
the church clocks around were striking eight we
came in sight of Bensington Lock. "*Mirabile
dictu*," we were not kept waiting, and accomplished our lock before daylight failed, getting
to Wallingford, our halting-place for the night,
soon afterwards. Wallingford is a curious old
town, with some Roman earthworks that look
like a rabbit warren, and a bit of an old castle
that is locked up in somebody's garden, and can't
be seen, though in its day it did good service for
Charles I.

About half-past ten the next morning I awoke
from a confused dream compounded of " Kay-
aks " and the falls of Niagara (this latter
ingredient being perhaps the offspring of the

L

foaming Weir at Bensington Lock), to the unpleasant consciousness that we ought to have
started an hour before ; that Easy had been up
for hours, and was in the state of mind usually
ascribed to *impastus leo ;* and that my minor
was still buried in oblivion and the bed-clothes.
However, soon after eleven we actually started,
to find the wind dead against us, and "way"
not nearly so easily made as on the previous day.
Having heard marvellous reports from a Walling-
fordian and the guide-book, about a certain
mineral spring *en route*, we stopped at a quaint
little apology for an inn, yclept " The Leather
Bottle," in order to see what effect its supposed
salubrious qualities would have on the *olla podrida*
in our heads of rhomboids, "variæ lectiones,"
historical facts and fiction and Greek particles,
the result of some three weeks' almost continu-
ous writing in the cause of certificates. Here
we were shown a grotto where the nymph of the
fountain was said to dwell; and to which a
flight of steps gave access. Down these Easy
boldly made his way ; the next moment, however, he must have forcibly realized the truth
of the words *facilis descensus Averni*, for without

any warning he suddenly found himself up to
his knees in the much-talked-of water, which
had formerly been in request all over the country side, though now it seemed to be used for no
other purpose than to entrap the unwary. Close
to "The Leather Bottle" are Ewing and Streatley;
the latter place famed for its soft and picturesque
scenery, as well as for its Roman road and ford.
Pangbourne Reach, too (about three miles further
down the river), as it appeared on that lovely
August morning, seemed " girt with a tranquil
glory," that made me wish I was artist enough
to sketch the natural beauties which might not
be there in such perfection on the morrow.

Between Mapledurham (one of the most
charming spots we passed) and Caversham, the
river runs parallel to the railway for some distance ; we passed Caversham Bridge, whence I
have started on many a water-party, about five,
and reached Sonning by 6.30. Here Easy
again deserted us, and went on to Henley,
having, as I said before, an idea that "twilight
on the Thames " and " malaria " were synony-
mous terms. We followed him about eight (my
minor cleverly contriving to leave his watch and

purse at the " French Horn," where we had tea),
and soon had reason to wish we had been his
companions, for it got gradually darker and
darker, until after passing Shiplake Lock we
could not see two yards in front of us. Half-an-
hour afterwards my minor startled me by declar-
ing we were going over the same bit of river we
had passed some time before ; and on throwing
a piece of white paper into the stream (it was
too dark to distinguish the current by any other
means), we discovered to our horror that we
must have turned round an eyot, and that we
had been going up stream again for about a mile.
At Marsh Lock we had two narrow escapes
from going down a mill-race, and over the weir,
before we found the narrow and labyrinthian lock
cut ; we did not reach Henley till 11.30, having
taken three hours and a half to do six miles.
By way of adding insult to the injury he had
done us by depriving us of his piloting aid,
Master Easy had thought fit to order no supper
for us : and having had his own very comfortably,
could afford to laugh at our objurgations at being
able to get nothing but bread and cheese. However, we paid him out by sleeping till eleven next

morning, and had a laugh at him below Hamble-
don Lock, where he and his canoe stuck on an
eel-basket in a vain attempt to "shoot" what at
first looked like a substantial rapid, but was in
reality only a very chimerical one. Soon after
this little episode, we passed Medmenham Abbey,
which in bygone years has enjoyed a good deal
of notoriety, sometimes not altogether of an
enviable nature ; indeed, in the last century it
was the rendezvous of a club whose motto of
" *Fay ceque Voudras*" sufficiently sets forth the
character of its members : however, whatever
the monasterial and social aspect of the abbey
was in days of yore, it has pleasant associations
for many an Etonian, for was it not the spot
where one of the most enjoyable camps in which
the Eton Corps ever took part was held in 1873 ?
The scenery of the river about here, especially
on the Medmenham side, is strongly suggestive
of that in some parts of the Wye, though perhaps
it is hardly so wild ; the long reach below Marlow, the Cookham Weir, the overhanging woods
of Cleveden, Maidenhead Bridge, in fact the
whole length of river between Marlow and Windsor, are too well known to Etonians to need

any description. Suffice it to say, we arrived at the well-known " raft " about six the third day after leaving Oxford, having thoroughly enjoyed ourselves.

LONDON :
GILBERT AND RIVINGTON, PRINTERS,
ST. JOHN'S SQUARE.

www.ingramcontent.com/pod-product-compliance
Lightning Source LLC
Chambersburg PA
CBHW021117020726
47500CB00003B/795